OUTLAW RANGER

VOLUME TWO

JAMES REASONER

WOLFPACK
PUBLISHING
— EST 2013 —

Outlaw Ranger, Volume Two
Print Edition
© Copyright 2021 (As Revised) James Reasoner

Wolfpack Publishing
5130 S. Fort Apache Rd. 215-380
Las Vegas, NV 89148

wolfpackpublishing.com

eBook ISBN 978-1-64734-766-6
Paperback ISBN 978-1-63977-027-4

OUTLAW RANGER

BLOOD AND GOLD

FRANCISCO GUZMAN WAS SCARED OF GHOSTS. HE KNEW they existed. His grandmother had told him many tales of how restless spirits wandered the earth, unable to find peace in their graves.

He could believe that many of them were roaming this canyon tonight, ready to take their spectral vengeance on anyone who dared to venture into the forbidding, high-walled passage.

Unfortunately, Barranca del Zopilote—Buzzard's Canyon, the gringos called it—was the quickest way to the settlement of Cemetery Butte and the smelter owned by Señor Martin Rainey. There were other routes from the mine in the mountains on the other side of the border but they would take the mules carrying the gold many miles out of their way. This, Señor Rainey would not allow. The sooner the gold was safely at the smelter, the better, as far as he was concerned.

Silvery moonlight washed down over the canyon from the glowing orb overhead. The steep walls cast impenetrable shadows along the sides and Francisco was convinced that was where the phantoms lurked.

The mule train, fourteen animals long, each loaded with several hundred pounds of ore, stayed in the center of the canyon where the light was better. One man led each mule. Francisco had the sixth one from the front. Six gringo guards on horseback accompanied the mule train: two riders in front, two behind, and one on each flank. They all moved as fast as they could. Señor Rainey feared that someone would try to steal his gold, so he insisted the ore be moved at night, as quickly as possible, straight from the mine to the smelter.

Steep cliffs rose along both sides of the Rio Grande for miles but the canyon provided a way through. It ran all the way to the river on the Mexican side and continued northward on the American side. When the river wasn't up from rains, which were quite rare here in West Texas, the mules could ford it easily.

And so, every month or so, the men loaded the mules and made this dash across the border...although since the mules were, well, mules, they didn't exactly dash.

Francisco had made two of these trips before and nothing had happened either time. That didn't really give him any confidence, though. The spirits could merely be waiting for the right moment to strike.

The bells hung from the mules' necks provided soft music for the scene. The steady clop of their hooves against the rocky canyon floor counterpointed the dissonant melody. None of it did anything to soothe Francisco's nerves.

A large, dark shape loomed up beside him, causing him to flinch. A man laughed and Francisco realized the shape was a man on horseback, the outrider on the left flank.

"Sort of jumpy there, aren't you, 'Cisco?" the man asked.

"Sí, Señor Evans," Francisco replied in the English he had learned from the priest in the village of Esperanza, downriver where his grandmother lived, where she had raised Francisco. "I do not like this place. I never have."

"I'm not all that fond of it myself," Ben Evans said. "It's sort of spooky-like."

"Sí," Francisco agreed fervently.

"The name don't help matters none. You know why it's called Buzzard's Canyon?"

"No, señor. Why?"

Evans laughed again and said, "Hell, I was hopin' you could tell me. I don't have any idea. But it must be because something died up in here sometime and folks saw buzzards circlin' over it."

"Something...or some*body*," Francisco muttered.

"Yeah, could be." Evans shook his head and went on, "Well, we're gettin' paid for takin' the gold through here, so I reckon that's all that really matters, isn't it?"

"Sí, señor," Francisco said again. It was true that he was getting paid.

He just wasn't getting paid *much*. Señor Rainey had not gotten to be a rich man by being generous to those he employed. Still, it was more than he could make trying to scratch out a living as a farmer.

A shout from up ahead made everyone stop. Carl Swann, one of the men leading the mule train, turned his horse and rode back to talk to Evans and the other flanker, Pete Jackson.

"Thought I spotted something up ahead," Swann said. "We'll hold the train right here for a minute while I go take a look."

5

"You're thinkin' it might be an ambush, Carl?" Evans asked.

"I dunno." Swann frowned which made his heavy-featured face look even more like a bulldog's. "I couldn't really tell what it was I saw. Something was there and, then all of a sudden, it wasn't."

Francisco crossed himself when he heard that, thinking again of restless spirits.

Swann pulled his Winchester from its saddle sheath and rode up the canyon. The other five guards pulled in closer to the mules and their valuable cargo.

Swann had been gone for less than a minute when gunfire erupted from atop the canyon walls. Something struck a smashing blow against Francisco's shoulder and knocked him against the mule he'd been leading. The mule jumped away skittishly and Francisco fell.

The blasts echoed back and forth in the canyon, mixing with shouted curses, cries of fear, and the screams of wounded animals. The riflemen on the heights didn't target the mules but they shot the horses out from under the guards. As Francisco struggled to sit up despite the pain that filled him, he saw Ben Evans thrown from the saddle as his mount went down.

Evans had yanked his rifle free as the horse staggered. He rolled, came up on one knee, and returned the fire, triggering half a dozen shots at the muzzle flashes on top of the eastern wall as fast as he could work the Winchester's lever. Then he surged to his feet, turned, and ran toward Francisco.

"'Cisco!" the man called. "Are you hit?"

Before Francisco could answer, Evans stopped short and arched his back. Francisco knew a bullet had just driven into the guard's body from behind. The next instant a shot struck Evans in the head. Something hot, wet, and sticky splattered over Francisco's face as the man collapsed right in front of him. He knew it was Evans' blood and brains he felt dripping down his cheeks.

He groaned and sagged back, sick with the knowledge that he was going to die here tonight, in this lonely, shadow-haunted canyon, just as he had feared.

It wasn't ghosts who had killed him, though. Ghosts didn't fire rifles.

The shooting continued for a while as Francisco drifted in and out of consciousness. Finally, he became aware that the gunfire had stopped. The canyon was quiet again except for the sighing of the wind that blew through it.

A few minutes later, he heard horses coming.

"Make sure they're all dead," a man ordered harshly.

Francisco was sick with pain from his wounded shoulder but somehow he retained enough presence of mind to realize that he might have a chance to survive this ambush after all. His face was covered with blood. He was sure he *looked* dead. If he could lie still enough, maybe the men would be convinced he was done for and wouldn't check his body closely...

"Well, that went off without a hitch," a familiar voice said.

Carl Swann.

Now Francisco understood why Swann had halted the mule train. He was making it easier for the thieves and killers to wipe out everyone else. He had sold out Señor Rainey and the rest of the men with the mule train.

"You did good, Carl," the other man said. Francisco was curious about him but didn't dare open his eyes. He lay there breathing so shallowly it would be difficult to see the rise and fall of his chest, especially in the uncertain moonlight.

"I earned my money, that's for damned sure," Swann said. "I drank and played cards with those men. It wasn't easy settin' 'em up to be killed like this."

"But you managed, didn't you?" the other man said in a mocking tone.

"Damn it, you got what you were after. Just gimme my money and let me get outta here. I want to put some miles behind me. When Martin Rainey realizes I'm the only one who survived, he'll know I sold him out. I want to be as far away as possible by then."

"Sure, you'll get what's coming to you."

"What—"

Swann didn't finish whatever he was about to say. The boom of a gunshot cut him off. Francisco had to open his eyes and look then. He saw a familiar figure topple out of the saddle and fall to the ground like a sack of wet sand.

"You had too much betrayal in your blood, Swann," the other man said as he slipped a revolver back in its holster. "Never could have trusted you not to talk."

A light footstep sounded close beside Francisco. He steeled himself not to react to it.

But it didn't matter. Someone said, "This one flinched when your gun went off."

It was a woman's voice.

"Look at me," she said.

Francisco was powerless to resist. His eyes were already open. His gaze swung over and, in the silvery moonlight, he saw the face of beauty.

And a gun. Flame gouted from the muzzle, and that was the last thing Francisco Guzman ever saw.

G.W. Braddock leaned forward, studied the chessboard for a long moment, then moved a knight.

"Believe that's check," he said.

The man in the brown robe on the other side of the table moved his king. Braddock gave chase with the knight but couldn't put the king in check again. The priest's queen swept all the way to the other side of the board and took Braddock's rook.

"And checkmate," the priest said.

Braddock laughed and said, "You did that on purpose. You lured me into a trap."

The priest cocked an eyebrow and said, "The object of the game, my friend." He smiled. "And it is good to hear you laugh. That is something I have not experienced very much."

That was true. Braddock's face had a naturally grim cast to it that wasn't helped by the scar running up his forehead and into his sandy brown hair. In the light of the candle that sat on a shelf in the priest's quarters at the mission, his lean features were deeply tanned which made the white scar stand out.

Even if his disposition hadn't been rather solemn to start with, the events of his recent life hadn't given Braddock much to laugh about. He had been a Texas Ranger, devoted to his job as a lawman, until a shake-up of the organization prompted by political foes had caused him to lose his badge.

That hadn't stopped him from continuing to hunt down the same sort of vicious owlhoots and killers he had brought to justice as a Ranger. He had no legal authority in the state of Texas or anywhere else. In fact, taking the law into his own hands, as he had done on several occasions, had made him into an outlaw in the eyes of the Rangers. At one point, his former boss, Captain John Hughes, had even sent men after him to arrest him.

They hadn't taken him into custody, though, and now he spent most of his time in the border village of Esperanza, on the southern side of the Rio Grande, where the priest had nursed him back to health after one of his adventures had left him gravely wounded. He was safe from capture here and the man of God had become Braddock's only real friend.

That wasn't enough to hold him, though, when he heard of injustice north of the border, of crimes that needed the attention of a Texas Ranger. The bullet-marked badge Braddock carried might not have any official standing anymore but, in his mind, that didn't remove his duty to deliver justice where it was needed.

"Another game?" the padre asked as he began putting the chess pieces back in their starting positions but, before Braddock could answer, a soft knock sounded on the door.

It was evening, time soon for Braddock to head back to the hut he had claimed as his own and the look of surprise on the priest's lined face indicated that he hadn't expected any other visitors. He got to his feet but Braddock uncoiled from his chair, too, and motioned for the padre to stay where he was.

Normally, Braddock didn't wear a gun while he was playing chess with the priest. He had taken off the gunbelt when he came in and hung it from a peg on the wall near the door. He went to it now and smoothly drew the Colt from its holster.

Esperanza was a peaceful village these days but it hadn't always been that way. Mexican bandits, American outlaws, and brutal Rurales all had taken their toll on the place and its inhabitants. Braddock had been in the middle of that violence and he might still have some enemies who had trailed him here. He wasn't going to take a chance on his friend opening the door to a bullet.

But when Braddock pulled the latch string and let the door swing open, he saw the visitor was no threat. The old woman who stood there caught her breath and took a step back as she saw the heavy revolver gripped in Braddock's strong brown hand.

Quickly, he lowered the gun and said, "I'm sorry, señora. I mean you no harm."

She crossed herself and told him, "You have frightened me out of years I cannot afford to lose, Señor Braddock!"

He recalled seeing her around the village but he didn't know her name. However, it was no surprise that she knew who he was. Everyone in Esperanza was aware of the grim-faced Texan now living in their midst.

The priest came up behind Braddock who stepped aside to let him smooth things over. While the priest ushered the woman in, Braddock slid the Colt back into leather.

"What can I do for you, Señora Dominguez?" the priest asked.

"I am here about my grandson," the old woman said. "The son of my daughter. Francisco."

"Of course. I remember Francisco. He went to work in the mines upriver, didn't he?"

"He did." Señora Dominguez drew in a deep breath. "But now he is dead."

"Dios Mio," the priest said under his breath. "Blessed Mother, what happened? An accident in the mine?"

He took the old woman's arm and steered her into the chair at the table where Braddock had been sitting earlier as they played chess. She sat there looking like she wanted to put her hands over her face and burst into tears but she was able to control herself.

She couldn't do anything about the pain that had settled deeply into her eyes, though. It looked like it would always be there.

"Francisco's death was no accident," she said. "He was killed. Murdered. Shot down like a dog from ambush, along with nine other men."

"How did this happen?" the priest asked.

"*Where* did this happen?" Braddock added.

The smile that had been on his face earlier was long gone now.

"Francisco, and the men with him, had taken a mule train across the Rio Grande, bound for the smelter in Cemetery Butte. The mules were carrying gold ore. The men were attacked in Barranca del Zopilote."

"Buzzard's Canyon," Braddock murmured.

"Sí," Señora Dominguez said, nodding. "It has always been known as a place of death. But it is the quickest way from Señor Rainey's mine in the mountains to his smelter in Texas."

"Rainey?" The name was vaguely familiar to Braddock.

"Martin Rainey," the priest supplied. "A rich man. And you know what the scripture says about a rich man."

"Easier for a camel to pass through the eye of a needle than for a rich man to enter the kingdom of Heaven." Braddock nodded. His mother had been a Bible-reading woman. The scriptures had never taken with his father whose only holy book had been the Rangers' "Bible", the list of wanted outlaws carried by every man who wore the silver star in a silver circle.

"I should say that I don't know Rainey or much about him," the padre went on. "Only his reputation which is that of a hard, ruthless man."

"To get back to the ambush," Braddock said to Señora Dominguez, "do you know exactly what happened?"

She shook her head and said, "Only that the men with the mule train were killed and the gold stolen. One of Francisco's friends from here in the village, who worked at the mine with him, came and told me." Now she couldn't hold back a sniffle. "The bodies...were taken to the gringo settlement...and buried. It was closer."

Unfortunately, in this climate, proximity was often the most important consideration in where someone who had died was laid to rest.

"I am truly sorry, señora," the priest said. "If you'd like, I can send word to Cemetery Butte and see if it would be possible to have Francisco's...remains...brought here and interred in our churchyard..."

She shook her head with surprising vehemence and said, "That would not change anything, padre. My only

13

living relative would still be dead. No..." She turned her head. "I came to see Señor Braddock."

Something began to stir inside Braddock. He had started to have an inkling of where this conversation was headed even before she turned that intent, dark-eyed gaze on him. Now, he was certain because he could see the thirst for vengeance shining in those eyes.

"You want me to find the men who did this terrible thing," he said quietly.

"Sí, señor. My Francisco must be avenged and so must the other men who were murdered."

The priest said, "El Señor Dios has told us that vengeance belongs to Him, señora, not to us here in this life."

"Then do not call it vengeance I seek. Call it justice."

"That's just what I was about to say," Braddock drawled.

"But Señor Braddock is no longer a—"

Braddock stopped the priest with a lifted hand.

"Some things never change, padre," he said. His hand strayed to his shirt pocket and, without thinking, he touched the object he carried there. He never pinned on the badge unless he crossed the Rio Grande but it was always with him.

"You understand," Señora Dominguez said. "You will do this thing."

It wasn't a question. There was no doubt in her voice.

"I'll leave first thing in the morning," he promised her.

The priest sighed and said, "I know there is small chance of talking you out of doing this, my friend, despite the danger."

"Not even a little bit," Braddock agreed.

"Where will you begin? Across the border?"

"That's where it happened. Seems like the place to

start is with this fella Rainey. He lives in Cemetery Butte?"

"He owns the whole town," the priest replied. "It is said his house there is the biggest between San Antonio and El Paso."

"Maybe he figures that's as close as he'll get to the kingdom of Heaven," Braddock said.

3

MARTIN RAINEY STARED INTO THE GLASS OF BRANDY FOR A second before he tossed the drink down his throat. He hadn't seen any answers in the liquor...but he hadn't really expected to find them there.

"Where's my son?" he asked.

The only other person in the room was Rainey's secretary, a slender, bespectacled man originally from Massachusetts named Charles Horner. He said, "The last time I saw Jason, he was headed down the trail toward town." Horner had lost most of his eastern accent. His words now held the soft drawl of the southwest.

"On his way to get drunk, no doubt."

"I wouldn't know about that."

"The hell you wouldn't, Charles," Rainey said. "You know more about what goes on up here on the butte and down in town than anybody else."

Horner cocked his head to the side and shrugged.

The house they were in was located on top of the butte that overlooked the settlement below. Rainey's

16

ranch, which was also the headquarters of his mining company, was the only thing on the butte other than the small, fence-enclosed graveyard about a mile away that gave the place its name. The settlement, established in the first place because it was on a freight wagon route, had been called Wooten starting out, after one of the men who'd founded it, but after the citizens had started burying folks up on the butte, they decided they liked the new name better. Old Wooten was one of those laid to rest in the rocky ground, so he didn't object.

Rainey went over to the sideboard, poured another drink. Horner said, "It's not noon yet, you know."

"I know what time it is. I don't care."

Horner shrugged again. If his boss wanted to get drunk before the sun reached its zenith, that was Rainey's business.

"If you see Jason later, tell him I want to talk to him."

Horner nodded and said, "Of course."

Rainey downed the drink.

It didn't do a damned thing to banish the image seared into his brain.

Dead men lying everywhere, covered with blood.

And his mules—along with his gold—gone.

JASON RAINEY WAS DRINKING at the same time as his father but instead of expensive brandy, he was tossing back cheap tonsil varnish in the Palomino Saloon.

Mounted on the front of the building, a wooden statue of a horse painted a golden color reared above the awning over the boardwalk. It was by far the fanciest thing about the Palomino.

It had been three days since the murderous ambush on the mule train but the settlement was still buzzing about the violence. Some of the guards who'd been killed had had friends here in town. When they gathered in the Palomino and the other saloons, they liked to talk about getting a posse together, crossing the border, and hunting down the bandidos who had committed this atrocity. Of course, so far, that was all it amounted to: talk.

A young woman with long red hair pulled back in a ponytail sidled up next to Jason. The paint on her face and the short, spangled dress made it plain what her profession was. She put a hand on Jason's arm, smiled at him, and said, "Sort of early for that, isn't it? If you want some comfort, I've got something better."

"You ain't my mother, Bess," Jason snapped. "My mother's dead a long time now."

"I know that," Bess said. "She died before you and your daddy ever came here, didn't she? That's what I've heard, anyway."

"Yeah. Before we came here. That's right."

Jason glared at the bartender and pointed at his empty glass. The man sighed and reached for the bottle.

"Come on upstairs with me," Bess urged as she rubbed a hand up and down Jason's arm. "I'll make you feel good."

"I reckon that's beyond your capabilities, darlin'..." Jason lifted the glass and swallowed the whiskey. "But I suppose it wouldn't hurt for you to try."

"Oh, I'll try real good," she promised as the two of them turned away from the bar.

The man who pushed through the batwings and stepped into the Palomino, at that moment, made Jason stop in his tracks.

18

The newcomer was tall, lean, and had the brim of his hat pulled low. A brown mustache framed lips that formed a taut line. He wore a holstered revolver which was becoming a more unusual sight in this modern, turn-of-the-century era, but it certainly wasn't unheard of.

The badge, though...They didn't show up much in this part of the country. Cemetery Butte had a marshal whose main duty was locking up the occasional drunk and letting him sleep it off. Since the county was bigger than a lot of eastern states, deputies from the sheriff's office didn't get down here to the border country very often. The main peacekeepers were the handful of hired guns who worked for Jason's father.

Jason had never seen a Texas Ranger in Cemetery Butte...until now.

When the man came closer, Jason saw there was something odd about the badge. It had a small hole in the center and, as Jason frowned, he thought that it looked for all the world like a bullet had punched through the metal. If that had been the case, though, the man who'd been wearing the badge ought to be dead. This hombre was very much alive although it appeared he'd taken some punishment in his time.

Bess tugged at Jason's arm and said, "Come on, hon. We got things to do."

"Hold on," Jason said. He was thinking rapidly. There was only one explanation for the Ranger's presence that made sense. Only one crime had been committed recently that would draw the attention of the law.

The man was here because of the attack on the mule train.

Jason shrugged off Bess's hand and said, "Go on now. I'll see you later, maybe."

She clutched at him again and said, "Damn it, Jason—"

She broke off with a little gasp as his hand closed tightly around her bare arm. His fingers dug into the soft flesh.

"I said go on," he told her between clenched teeth.

Quite a few pale freckles dusted her cheeks and nose. They seemed to darken but it was really the color washing out of her face. She swallowed, jerked her head in a nod, and said, "Sure, Jason. Sure."

He let go of her. She stepped back. Her other hand went to her arm to rub lightly where he had grabbed it.

Jason had already forgotten about her completely as he moved away from the bar and planted himself in the Ranger's path.

———

BRADDOCK NODDED to the husky young man who stood in front of him. Thick blond curls were visible under the man's thumbed-back hat. His clothes were good although they looked like the man didn't really take care of them very well.

The youngster said, "You're a Texas Ranger."

Braddock smiled thinly and said, "That's why I'm wearing the badge."

That was why he would always wear it, whether his name was on the official rolls or not. What a man *was* didn't depend on somebody else agreeing with it.

"You're here about that ambush in Buzzard's Canyon."

It wasn't a question, so Braddock didn't bother answering it. Instead, he said, "I'm here because I've been on the trail for a while and I could use something to cut the dust."

Actually, Braddock had stopped at the Palomino because it was the biggest saloon in town and he figured people would be talking about the ambush and robbery. Nothing else like that had happened in these parts lately or maybe ever. It wouldn't hurt anything to pick up some gossip before he went to see Martin Rainey.

He had already taken note of the big, three-story, whitewashed house perched atop the butte just north of town and knew that was where he would find Rainey unless the man had an office down here in town. He could find that out by asking in the saloon, too.

"I'll buy you a beer," the young man said. He turned and gestured to the bartender. "Draw a beer and put it on my tab, Hank."

The drink juggler bobbed his balding head and said, "Sure, Mr. Rainey."

Braddock kept his face impassive but, inside, he was a little surprised to hear the name. This big, handsome youngster didn't look like the sort of man to own a successful ranch north of the line and a lucrative gold mine in the mountains south of the border.

"You're Martin Rainey?" Braddock asked.

"What?" The man shook his head. "Hell, no. That's my father. I'm Jason Rainey."

He stuck out his hand.

Braddock gripped it and said, "G.W. Braddock." It was doubtful anybody would recognize his name. The Rangers would have kept any mention of his activities out of the newspapers. Having somebody going around doing their job for them would be an embarrassment.

Jason Rainey picked up the beer and used his other hand to wave at an empty table in the back corner of the room.

"Let's sit down," he suggested. "I'll tell you all about the old man."

This was too good an opportunity for Braddock to pass up. He said, "I'm much obliged," and he didn't just mean for the beer.

4

"My father was a major in the army," Jason began as he leaned back in his chair and stretched his legs under the table. "He fought the Apaches in Arizona Territory and dragged my mother and me from one dusty outpost to another. She tried to tell him that sort of life wasn't good for her. Her health was never the best. He didn't really listen to her, though. It took her dying for him to understand."

"I'm sorry," Braddock said.

Jason spread his hands and shook his head.

"You can't hold a man's ambition against him. My father had his sights set on being a general. He would have been a good one, too."

"But he left the army?"

Jason nodded and said, "Yeah." He picked up the glass of whiskey he had brought to the table with him and sipped from it, rather than downing the whole shot. "He'd inherited some land here in Texas from an old bachelor uncle. We didn't know it was a ranch, and a pretty good one, until we got here. He bought some cattle from a man who had a spread below the border, Felipe Santiago. Santiago owned a gold mine in the mountains, too, but it never had paid off much and was about to go broke. He still believed it was just a matter of time until they struck a lode, though, so he talked my father into going partners with him." Jason took another drink. "It wasn't six months before they hit that lode and they've been taking gold out of the tunnel ever since."

"Making your father a rich man."

"Yep. His luck turned when he left the army."

Braddock swallowed some of the beer which was no better and no worse than what you'd find in most frontier saloons. Mostly, it was just wet. He said, "Why are you telling me all this, Jason?"

"Well, you came here to track down the men who ambushed that mule train and killed those poor fellas, didn't you?"

"That's right."

"I figured you'd need to know some of the background. Might help you figure out who'd want to hurt my father by hitting that train."

Braddock's eyes narrowed. He said, "You think stealing all that gold ore bound for the smelter wasn't good enough reason?"

"Well, sure, but there could have been more to it than that."

"Like what?"

Jason polished off the drink and said, "Like Felipe Santiago died a while back...after my father had finagled him out of his share of the mine."

Braddock's eyebrows went up. He couldn't stop them. He said, "Your father stole Santiago's half of the mine?"

"I wouldn't say *stole*," Jason replied with a shrug. "Rustlers had been hitting Santiago's herds hard for a while. He needed money. My father bought out Santiago's share of the mine for less than it was worth but Santiago wasn't in any position to haggle. Then he wound up losing the ranch anyway. It didn't help matters that he wasn't on good terms with the political powers that be down there."

Braddock nodded slowly. He understood all too well about how politics could ruin a man's life.

"So your father wound up with everything and Santiago got nothing."

"He died a broken man," Jason said. "And he left behind a son who blames it all on my pa. Manuel Santiago's been helling around below the border making noises about how he was going to settle the score for his father."

"So you think he might have had something to do with bushwhacking that mule train?"

"He knew the route my father's been using to transport the ore," Jason said.

"I imagine plenty of other people around here did, too."

"Yeah, sure, but Manuel used to work in the mine office down there. He knew about how long it was between shipments, so he could make a pretty good guess when one would be going out. He knew my father likes to move the gold at night, too." Jason made a face and shook his head. "He thinks it's safer. I tried to tell him the shadows just give bandits more places to hide, but he doesn't seem to see it that way."

Braddock drank more of the beer and said, "You may be on to something there but suspicion is a long way from proof. I'll still need to talk to your father."

"Shoot, yeah. I'll take you up there myself and introduce you to the old man."

"Thanks." Braddock paused. "You say Manuel Santiago worked in the mine office?"

"That's right."

"What do you do, if you don't mind me asking."

Jason grinned, waved a hand to indicate the interior of the Palomino, and said, "You're lookin' at it."

THE HUGE BUILDING that housed the smelter and stamp mill was quiet at the moment. No smoke came from its stacks. It stood at the edge of the settlement as silent and unmoving as a monument.

When it was working, its roar would fill the air and people would feel the vibrations from its machinery through their feet as they went about their daily tasks. It was what brought life to the town of Cemetery Butte, along with the Spade Ranch which was also owned by Martin Rainey. His money was the blood in the settlement's veins.

In Braddock's time as a Ranger, he had seen other places like this, places dependent for their very existence on one man. Usually, they weren't very happy places because the people who lived there knew everything they had relied on the whims of a single individual. That bred a certain powerlessness in people.

And powerlessness bred resentment.

Somebody who wanted to strike back at Martin Rainey probably wouldn't have much trouble recruiting men to help him. Most rich men had an abundance of enemies to go along with their wealth.

Those thoughts went through Braddock's mind as he rode up the trail to the top of the butte with Jason Rainey. Braddock's dun was a rangy animal, not much for looks, but it had sand and could run all day. Jason's mount, a big roan, was much more impressive, and Jason cut a splendid figure atop the animal.

The sides of the butte sloped down fairly gently. The trail didn't even have to zigzag back and forth. It just climbed straight from the plains to the top. It didn't feel to Braddock like they were very high until he turned slightly in his saddle when they were almost there and looked back to the south, toward the Rio Grande several miles distant and the rugged mountains beyond the river. The landscape spread out before him like a painting in hues of brown and tan and gray with bursts of green vegetation here and there.

"What made folks decide to start burying their loved ones up here?" he mused. "The view?"

"Could be," Jason said. "The town's graveyard was already on top of the butte when my father and I came to these parts. You're right, though, that the scenery is pretty impressive. The air's so clear that when you stand on the gallery of my father's house it looks almost like you can reach out across the river and touch those mountains."

The trail branched at the top. To the right, Jason explained, was the cemetery, about half a mile away. The path that curved to the left led to the Spade Ranch. Braddock could see the house from where they were, along with the outbuildings and the corrals.

"I'm not sure I'd like living in a house that close to the edge," he said.

"Well, it's not like it's on a cliff," Jason said, smiling. "The drop-off's not sheer. It can't collapse in an avalanche or anything like that. But from the second floor balcony, it does seem like the world sort of drops out from under you. You get used to it, though. Hell, a man can get used to anything."

Braddock wasn't so sure about that but he wasn't going to argue.

The house had a covered porch that ran around all four sides. Given the relative scarcity of trees in this part of the country, the lumber to build such a place must have cost a fortune. Braddock asked, "Was the house here before you and your father moved in?"

That question brought a laugh from Jason. He said, "Not hardly. I told you, Great-uncle Jesse was a bachelor. He lived in a little shack and that was enough for him. And that was where my father and I lived until the gold strike. Then he built the house. Said it was the sort of place my mother would have liked." He shrugged and added, "Seems like a waste to me, her being gone and all, but there's no arguing with my father."

A man came out onto the porch as Braddock and Jason rode up to one of several hitch rails located around the house. He wore glasses and a gray tweed suit and said, "Your father wants to see you, Jason."

"I'm sure you told him I'd gone down to town, didn't you, Mr. Horner?"

The man's face got a dour look on it. He said, "I didn't lie to him if that's what you mean."

"I wouldn't expect you to."

Horner frowned at Braddock as the two riders swung down from their saddles and looped reins around the hitch rails.

"Who's this?"

"Can't you see the badge?" Jason asked. "This man's a Texas Ranger, come to track down the bastards responsible for what happened in Buzzard's Canyon."

The man came down the three steps from the porch

to the ground and extended his hand. He said, "I'm Charles Horner, Mr. Rainey's secretary."

"G.W. Braddock," the Ranger said as he gripped Horner's hand.

The door Horner had come out of a few moments earlier banged back against the wall as a man stepped onto the porch and said in a loud, angry voice, "By God, Jason, can't you at least wait until the middle of the day to start your drinking and tomcatting around?"

5

MARTIN RAINEY LOOKED LIKE THE MILITARY MAN HE HAD once been, thought Braddock. Tall, ramrod-spined, with graying hair and a neatly trimmed mustache. He wore a white shirt, black trousers and vest, and string tie and managed to make the outfit look like a uniform.

"You're a fine one to talk," Jason said. "I'll bet you've been in the brandy already this morning."

"Watch your tongue," Rainey snapped. His gaze swung to Braddock. "Is that a Ranger badge I see on your shirt, sir?"

"That's right," Braddock said. "G.W. Braddock's the name."

Charles Horner put in, "Ranger Braddock is here to investigate the robbery."

"And the murders of the men with the mule train," Braddock said.

"Of course. That goes without saying."

Maybe Horner thought so but Braddock didn't feel the same way. The killing of Francisco Guzman was what had brought him here and his main goal was to deliver justice to whoever was responsible for that and the deaths of the other men with the mule train. If he recovered Martin Rainey's gold in the process, that was all well and good but it wasn't his first priority.

Rainey put aside his annoyance with his son and nodded to Braddock. He said civilly enough, "I'm glad to see you, sir. I'm a bit puzzled, however. I didn't send word to the Rangers and ask for help."

"You didn't have to. News of a massacre like that gets around in a hurry."

"I suppose." Rainey held out a hand toward the door. "Come inside and we'll talk. I'm sure you have a great many questions. And, of course, you'll stay for dinner."

"Thank you."

Jason said, "You won't need me." He turned away and called to a wrangler who had just come out of the barn with another man. "Claude, come get my horse."

While the wrangler did that, Jason walked toward the bunk house. The other man who had come out of the barn moved to join him. Braddock glanced at that man, then looked again when he realized that he knew the hombre's face.

Happy Jack Conover, so called because nobody could remember ever seeing the gunman crack a smile.

Conover was suspected in a number of killings, including some back-shootings, as well as other crimes, Braddock recalled, but there were no formal charges against the man in Texas unless they had been filed recently. It was hard to figure what Conover was doing here on Martin Rainey's ranch. He was no cowboy, that was for sure.

Maybe Conover was one of the men Rainey had hired to guard the gold shipments but hadn't been along on the trip through Buzzard's Canyon.

"Ranger Braddock?"

Rainey's voice broke into Braddock's musing. Braddock turned and muttered, "Sorry."

He followed Rainey into the house, glancing back once to see Jason and Conover going into the bunk house together, talking animatedly as they did so.

Rainey led Braddock into a comfortably furnished parlor and offered him a drink and a cigar, both of which Braddock refused politely. They sat down in armchairs and Braddock dropped his hat on the floor beside him. He said, "Tell me about what happened in that canyon three nights ago."

Grim-faced, Rainey told the story, most of which Braddock already knew. When the mule train didn't show up at the smelter on time, Rainey and some of his men rode for the canyon and found the bodies of the slain mine workers and guards there, along with the guards' horses that had been shot out from under them. The mules and their packs full of gold ore were gone.

"It's just a guess, of course, since there weren't any survivors to tell us exactly what happened but, from the looks of it, the thieves posted riflemen on top of the canyon walls. There was considerable moonlight that night, so it probably wasn't too difficult to target the men with the mule train."

"I haven't seen the place myself but it sounds like it's tailor-made for an ambush."

Rainey's mouth already had a grim cast. It tightened even more as he said, "There's no way to get the gold from the mine to here without running some risks and that canyon is the shortest, fastest route. It's always seemed to me that the less time it takes to move the gold, the safer it is for everybody."

Braddock shrugged slightly. Rainey had a point, he

supposed. He asked, "Did you try tracking the thieves the next day?"

"We did. I'm not a bad tracker, if I do say so myself. I have some experience from my days in the army, fighting the Apache."

"I heard about that," Braddock said with a nod. "Your son mentioned it."

"He probably said a number of other things as well. Jason has never learned to keep his mouth shut, whether it's foolish words coming out or rotgut whiskey going in."

Braddock steered the conversation back on track by asking, "What did you find when you went after them?"

"The trail led toward the border, of course. Like most of the lawless element around here, they sought refuge in Mexico. We followed them but lost the trail a mile or so south of the Rio. It's rugged country over there. Difficult for tracking."

Braddock nodded, then asked, "All the men with the mule train were shot from ambush?"

"That's right." Rainey grimaced. "Although it appeared that a few of them survived the initial volley and were finished off at close range. A few of them had powder burns on their clothing. One young man was shot in the face from not far away, poor devil." Rainey blew out an angry breath between his teeth. "His eyes were still open."

"That's pretty brutal."

"Indeed. I'm not the mercenary monster you might imagine, Ranger. I don't just care about the gold I lost. I want you to find those men so they'll pay for the killing they did."

"That's what I'm here for. Tell me about the men who were with the mule train."

"Well, the workers were all Mexican, of course." Rainey's tone had a casualness to it that rubbed Braddock the wrong way but he tried not to show it. Rainey went on, "The man in charge of the guards that night was Carl Swann. A good man, quite competent and reliable."

Braddock knew the name. Swann was considered to have been on the wrong side of the law in the past but, like Conover, he wasn't wanted in Texas as far as Braddock knew.

"The other men were cut from the same cloth," Rainey went on. He named them and Braddock recognized several of those names, too. They were hired gunmen, hardcases but not actual outlaws.

"Sounds like the men who ride for you are pretty tough," he commented.

Rainey jerked his head in a nod and said, "They have to be. I don't care if it *is* the Twentieth Century, this is still rough country out here, Ranger. It hasn't changed much in the past thirty years except that the Apaches have all moved across the border and don't raid much anymore. But it still takes hard men to survive." His mouth twitched. "No offense, but there isn't much law in these parts."

"Texas is a big state," Braddock said, "and there aren't enough Rangers to go around."

Especially now, when the force had been reduced to a shadow of the Frontier Battalion it had once been. And that was why there was a need for a man like him...

He went on, "Do you know anybody who might have a grudge against you, Mr. Rainey? Somebody who might try to strike back at you by killing your men and stealing that gold?"

Rainey shook his head and said blandly, "No, I can't think of anyone like that."

34

"I understand you used to have a partner in the mine..."

Rainey leaped to his feet and exclaimed, "That insolent young pup!"

In a cool voice, Braddock asked, "Are you talking about your son...or Manuel Santiago?"

Rainey stared at him for a second, then said, "I was talking about Jason but the description applies to Manuel, too. Jason had no business gossiping about family matters to you, Ranger, and Manuel is just flat wrong. I never set out to hurt his father. I did everything I could for Felipe and when he died I would have taken care of Manuel and his sister if he'd let me."

Rainey stopped, heaved a sigh, and scrubbed a hand over his face. An air of weariness suddenly gripped the man.

"What did Jason tell you?" he asked.

"That you bought Santiago's share of the mine after rustlers almost ruined his ranch," Braddock said. "That you paid him less than what it was worth because he was desperate. And then Santiago lost everything anyway."

"That mine is a business, not a charity," Rainey said. "Felipe's ranch was more important to him. He was determined to hang on to it. I paid him as much as any canny businessman would have for his part. There's no shame in making a shrewd deal."

"And it didn't occur to you that Manuel Santiago might blame you for his father's death? That he could have tried to settle the score with you by stealing that gold and murdering your men?"

Rainey sagged back into his chair and muttered, "I suppose I thought about it. How could I not? I've heard rumors about the things he says about me in the cantinas down there. But I don't want to believe it.

There was a time when the boy was almost like a second son to me."

"Do you know where I might find him?"

"Not on this side of the border." Rainey let out a curt bark of laughter. "But then, you Rangers don't always let little things like borders stop you, do you?"

Braddock didn't reply but what Rainey said was true. Most Rangers would cross the Rio Grande in pursuit of a known outlaw.

Manuel Santiago didn't fall into that category, though. Braddock might suspect him but he didn't have any proof.

Of course, given his situation, he was even more inclined to bend the law to achieve justice than the regular Rangers were.

"The closest settlement to the old Santiago ranch is Alamoros," Rainey said after a moment. "That's where Manuel spends most of his time, from what I hear. Are you going after him?"

"I'll conduct my investigation in the way I see fit," Braddock answered.

"All right. I want those killers brought to justice, no matter where the trail leads you."

"That's just what I plan on," Braddock said.

6

THE MIDDAY MEAL, SERVED BY THE MEXICAN COOK AND housekeeper, was good but Braddock didn't pay much attention to the taste of the food. His mind was occupied by thoughts of what had happened in Buzzard's Canyon and what he had learned about those gruesome events.

Jason didn't join Braddock and Rainey for the meal but Charles Horner did. Idly curious, Braddock asked about the secretary's background.

"I come from Massachusetts," Horner said. "My older brother served with Mr. Rainey in Arizona."

"He was my adjutant," Rainey said. "A fine man and a fine soldier. After he was killed by those savages, I stayed in touch with his family. That's how Charles came to work for me."

"I don't like to dwell on the past," Horner said. "How do you plan to proceed with your investigation, Ranger Braddock?"

"I figured I'd ride down to this Buzzard's Canyon and take a look around," Braddock said. "I know you already trailed the killers from there but sometimes a fresh set of eyes might see something else, even after a few days."

Rainey nodded and said, "I can send some of the men with you."

"I'd rather you didn't," Braddock said bluntly. "I'll check it out on my own."

"Of course. Whatever you'd prefer."

When they had finished eating, Braddock and Rainey went out onto the front porch again. Braddock paused at the top of the steps and looked toward the bunk house where Jason and Happy Jack Conover had disappeared earlier.

"Those rustlers who ruined Felipe Santiago," Braddock said, "were they ever caught?"

"Not that I'm aware of. There's no shortage of bandits below the border, however. It could have been almost anyone who stole all those cattle from Felipe."

"I suppose so," Braddock said.

He couldn't help but think, though, about how one of the crimes laid at the feet of Happy Jack Conover in the past was rustling.

The man was rumored to be a top-notch widelooper. So good, in fact, that he had never been caught at it.

———

BRADDOCK HAD plenty to think about as he rode toward Buzzard's Canyon.

During the ride up here from Esperanza, he had assumed that the outlaws who killed Martin Rainey's men and stole his gold were just run-of-the-mill owlhoots— maybe more vicious than some—and interested only in the valuable cargo being carried by the mules.

Now, it appeared that he might have stumbled into something deeper than that. Rainey must have known his partner Felipe Santiago well. He could have guessed that if Santiago's ranch was threatened, the man would grasp at any straw to save it, including letting Rainey buy him out for much less than his share of the mine was worth.

It was a big jump from there to thinking Rainey had had something to do with the rustling that broke Santiago...but Rainey had a known rustler in Happy Jack Conover on his payroll. Some of the other men who worked for Rainey were probably just as shady as Conover was.

If that ugly suspicion had reared up in Braddock's mind, it certainly could have in Manuel Santiago's. Manuel might even have evidence linking Rainey to the rustling.

If he did, the question was what would Braddock do about it? Even if Rainey was guilty of that, it didn't justify the murders of twenty men and the theft of all that gold ore. Those crimes had been committed in Texas. The rustling of Felipe Santiago's cattle had taken place across the line in Mexico.

Thinking about it put a frown on Braddock's face. There was law and there was justice and the two things weren't always the same. But regardless of the reason, he couldn't overlook mass murder. At the same time, if he was right about Conover and some of Rainey's other hired guns being the rustlers, then Rainey bore his share of responsibility for what had happened, too.

Braddock gave a little shake of his head as he reached the head of Buzzard's Canyon and reined in. He had followed the directions Rainey had given him and found the canyon with no trouble. Now he leaned forward in the saddle and studied it.

The trail dropped into the canyon at a fairly steep angle but horses and mules would be able to manage the slope without any trouble. It ran for several miles to the Rio Grande and continued southward on the far side of the border river. As the trail dropped down, rocky bulwarks reared up on either side of it. The ground was uneven and littered with boulders that provided plenty of hiding places for bushwhackers.

Braddock turned the dun away from the trail and rode along the left-hand canyon wall instead, weaving around the ridges and big slabs of rock. He kept his eyes open and he was about halfway to the river when he spotted the afternoon sun gleaming on something. He reined in, swung down from the saddle, and picked up an empty brass cartridge case.

The case was from a standard .44-40 cartridge, Braddock saw, the sort of ammunition used by countless Winchesters. Meaningless when you thought about how many men in this part of the country carried rifles of that caliber.

Braddock's gut told him, though, that this particular rifle was one of those used to massacre the men with the mule train. He squinted and studied the end of the cartridge closely. The rifle's firing pin was off just the tiniest bit, he saw from the markings on the case. It was unlikely he'd be able to match this cartridge to the rifle that had fired it, assuming he ever found the weapon, but it was at least possible.

He stuck the cartridge case in his pocket and continued searching the rim.

He didn't find anything else on either canyon wall except a few stray hoofprints. The ground was too hard to take tracks well and there was no way of knowing if the prints he found belonged to the killers' horses.

Braddock rode down into the canyon then. A hot wind was blowing from the south and it whistled a little as it moved between the high, rocky walls. The sound was a mournful one. Despite the sunshine, an aura of gloom seemed to hang over the canyon.

Braddock told himself that was all in his mind. He wasn't the most imaginative sort and he knew it but, in recent months, he had been given to occasional fits of melancholy. That was all this was, he thought. The canyon had a sinister reputation to start with or else it wouldn't have been named what it was. The knowledge that a score of men had died here only a few nights earlier made it worse.

He put that out of his thoughts. He was here to do a job and brooding wasn't part of it. Instead, he ranged back and forth across the canyon as he worked his way toward the Rio Grande, searching for anything that might tell him something about the men who had carried out this atrocity.

The bodies of men and horses had been removed, of course, and Braddock didn't know exactly where in the canyon the mule team was when the attack took place. Somewhere in the center, though, he'd been told, and he paused there to look back and forth at the walls.

At night, even with plenty of moonlight, it wouldn't be easy to hit a target from up there. But if the bush-whackers just poured lead down into the canyon, the men caught in that deadly crossfire would fall sooner or later. Braddock was a little surprised none of the mules had been killed. The stolid beasts of burden had been lucky.

He was sitting there contemplating the wall on the

eastern side of the canyon when sunlight suddenly glinted off something up there. The reflection stabbed at him, warning him.

Braddock reacted instantly, throwing himself forward on the dun's neck as he jammed his heels against the horse's flanks. Something hummed over Braddock's back as the dun leaped ahead.

A split-second later he heard the flat crack of a rifle, followed by another shot and the wicked whine of a bullet ricocheting off a rock.

Well, he asked himself, *what did you expect in a place with a name like this one has?*

The buzzards might soon have good reason to circle overhead once again.

7

Braddock hauled the dun around and sent it galloping toward the eastern wall. He knew he would present a more difficult target heading toward the hidden rifleman, rather than away from him. He angled the horse a little from side to side. Bullets kicked up dirt and gravel around them, but luck was on their side.

Braddock raced into the rocks along the base of the wall. The bushwhacker didn't have a very good angle on them now. He would have to fire almost straight down at them.

As Braddock kicked his feet from the stirrups, he hauled his Winchester from its saddle sheath. He hit the ground running and moved away from the dun. The rifle had fallen silent but, if there was any more shooting, he wanted to draw it away from the horse.

He stopped next to one of the boulders, jacked the Winchester's lever, and craned his neck to peer up at the rimrock. Nothing was moving up there against the pale blue sky.

Another shot ripped through the afternoon air but

this one came from the other side of the canyon. The bullet *spanged* off the boulder only a few feet from Braddock, throwing rock dust in his face. He grated a curse and moved quickly around the boulder to put it between him and the rifleman on the far side of the canyon.

They had him pinned down good and proper, he thought disgustedly.

And yet he couldn't complain too much, he thought. In the back of his mind, on the way down here to the canyon, had been the thought that someone might follow him. That was why he hadn't made his presence in Cemetery Butte a secret. If anybody connected to the killers was still around these parts, having a Texas Ranger poking into the massacre might spook them into doing something reckless...like trying to bushwhack him.

Why chase outlaws when he could make them come to him?

Now the trick would be to survive somebody taking that bait.

Braddock took off his hat and held it in his left hand as he edged his head around the boulder. He didn't see any movement on the far wall of the canyon which was about a hundred and fifty yards away at this point. A fairly long shot but, certainly, not out of rifle range for a keen-eyed marksman. The bullet coming so close to him proved that.

A grating sound from above him made him pull back quickly and look up at the rimrock. There were boulders up there, too, he recalled. Suddenly, he felt a cold ball of fear in his belly.

He saw something dark loom against the sky. That gunman on the other side of the canyon probably had his rifle lined up, just waiting to fire, but Braddock knew he couldn't stay here, despite that. He broke into a run along the base of the wall. Instinct, made him dive forward.

The huge rock that plummeted down behind him missed by only a few feet. With a thunderous crash that shook the earth, it struck where Braddock had been standing.

Braddock landed hard, lost both his hat and his rifle. The impact knocked the breath out of him and left him stunned for a second. The echoes from the boulder falling rolled through the canyon. Shots boomed from the far side, mixing with the echoes. Bullets hit the ground close to Braddock and spewed gravel in his face.

The stinging sensations from that gravel goaded him into movement. He pushed himself onto hands and knees, grabbed his hat and Winchester, and surged to his feet. He ran again. Another rock crashed down behind him, smaller this time but still big enough to have broken his head open like a melon if it had landed on him.

He thought about swinging the rifle up and spraying lead toward the far wall but that would be just a waste of ammunition, he decided. Hurried shots at this range, fired on the run, would have no chance of hitting anything. He concentrated on running instead, something his high-heeled boots weren't made for.

There were more rocks ahead where he could take cover from the rifleman on the other side of the canyon, but that would still leave him vulnerable to attacks from above.

A thought popped into Braddock's mind. Abruptly, he reversed course and angled out into the canyon. That put him more at risk from the rifleman but, with danger all around him, he didn't see that he had any choice. This gave him the best chance of disposing of one of the threats.

He stopped and turned his back on the man trying to shoot him. That made his skin crawl. He expected to feel a bullet smash into him at any second. But he ignored the sensation as best he could and brought his Winchester to his shoulder as he scanned the rimrock above and ahead of him.

There! The man who had been trying to crush him under the rocks had run ahead to another boulder and had his shoulder against it, rocking it a little and working it toward the edge. The rifle in Braddock's hand cracked. The man yelled and twisted as the slug ripped through him. He stumbled toward the brink and clawed at the pistol holstered on his hip.

He didn't get the gun out. A scream erupted from him as he lost his balance, toppled off the edge, and plunged toward the ground forty feet below. The scream cut off with an ugly thud.

Braddock felt a bullet sizzle past his ear. He sprinted for the rocks again. Shots whined off the boulders as he threw himself behind them.

So far, it seemed like there were only two bush-whackers, one on each side of the canyon. If that was true, he had just doubled his chances of getting out of here alive.

From where he crouched now, he could see the crumpled body of the man he had shot. The man was lying on his side, facing away from Braddock, so the Ranger couldn't get a good enough look to recognize him.

Braddock's heart slugged harder in his chest as he heard that ominous grinding and scraping again. Some-body else *was* up there above him, and they were shoving another boulder toward the edge.

The sounds weren't coming from directly above him,

however, and as he jerked his head up to gaze toward the rimrock, he saw why. One of the rocks perched near the brink rocked back and then forward and then overbalanced enough to topple off. It shot down through the air—

And landed on the ambusher Braddock had killed.

Braddock grimaced and air hissed between his teeth as he saw blood spurt out around the boulder. The echoes of its fall bounced back and forth in the canyon, then faded to be replaced by a tense silence. The man on the other wall had stopped shooting.

A pair of legs stuck out from under the boulder, but that was all. The dead man's head and torso were crushed to a red paste, Braddock knew. There would be no way of identifying him.

Braddock pondered what that might mean and, as he did, he heard the swift rataplan of hoofbeats from the other side of the canyon.

From the sound of it, the bushwhacker over there was lighting a shuck.

Had the second man on this side called off the ambush? Braddock didn't know but it seemed likely. The possibility got even stronger a few moments later when he heard rapid hoofbeats from the wall above him. They faded quickly.

Braddock waited, unwilling to emerge from cover just yet in case the bushwhackers were trying to trick him. Long minutes stretched out as a buzzing sound began to fill the air. Flies were gathering around the pool of blood spreading from under the boulder.

Finally, with his Winchester held ready, Braddock stepped out into the open. He looked across the canyon and at the rimrock above him and saw no sign of movement. The sunlight didn't reflect off any gun barrels.

The would-be killers were gone.

Although Braddock was convinced of that, he didn't let his guard down as he retrieved his hat and then stepped over to the last boulder that had fallen. The blood on the ground around it had an oily sheen that made his stomach clench slightly. As he approached, flies rose from the crimson pool and swarmed in the air. Braddock waved his hat to scatter them.

He could have tried to find a branch so he could lever the big rock off its victim, or used his rope and the dun to try to drag it off, but the whole idea seemed pointless. He wasn't going to recognize what was left of the man. The bastard's mother wouldn't know him now.

He studied the protruding legs for a moment, though. They were clad in denim jeans and the boots on the feet were well-worn, nothing fancy, just the sort of boots that any cowboy on this range might wear. Plain spurs were strapped on them.

Actually, all this told him was who the dead man *wasn't*. He could rule out Martin and Jason Rainey and Charles Horner, all of whom were better dressed than this hombre. He didn't know of a reason why any of those three would want to kill him, either.

A slight frown creased Braddock's forehead. If Manuel Santiago really was to blame for the massacre, it was possible he had spies in Cemetery Butte who could have alerted him to Braddock's presence. Santiago could have sent men up here to keep an eye on the canyon and kill anybody who came snooping around.

But Mexican vaqueros tended to favor gaudier spurs than that, Braddock thought. It wasn't a hard-and-fast rule, of course, but his hunch was that the dead man was a gringo.

The only thing he knew for sure was that somebody

didn't like him being here. The killers had to be afraid that he would uncover their identities.

That told him the best thing to do was to keep poking, although it meant he would be wearing a target on his back.

It wouldn't be the first time, he thought wryly.

A whistle brought the dun trotting up the canyon toward him. Braddock was glad to see that the horse was unharmed. He swung into the saddle and headed south toward the border.

8

ALAMOROS WAS MORE THAN A VILLAGE FULL OF FARMERS. It was a good-sized settlement with a business district that stretched for three blocks and quite a few adobe houses on the cross streets. A large mission with a tall bell tower stood at the far end of the main street. The bell in it was tolling the arrival of evening as Braddock rode in.

His badge was back in his pocket. It had no standing here. Other than being a target, it didn't mean anything to anyone except him. And he knew it was always there whether he wore it or not.

Being a gringo, he would stand out here but, no doubt, there were other Americans in this settlement as well. Men drifted across the border from Texas for all sorts of reasons. Most were on the run, either from the law or from something else in their lives.

Braddock reined the dun to a stop in front of a large adobe building with *FLORES CANTINA* painted above its entrance which had batwing doors across it just like an American saloon. He dismounted and looped the reins around a hitch rail where several other horses were tied. In the fading light, he saw that most of them carried the "skillet of snakes" brands popular south of the border, meaning they probably belonged to vaqueros.

One horse had a more familiar brand on it, though: a shovel-like shape that Braddock knew represented the Spade Ranch. Martin Rainey's ranch. Braddock had seen it on Jason Rainey's horse that morning as they rode to the top of Cemetery Butte.

That was interesting but didn't mean anything yet. Rainey had business interests south of the Rio Grande, so it made sense that one of his men might be down here. In fact, from what Braddock knew of the geography, Rainey's mine was only a few miles from here.

Quite a bit of noise came from the cantina, a blend of guitar music, laughter, and talk. None of it slowed down when Braddock pushed the batwings apart and walked into the room. Everyone seemed to ignore him.

The hair on the back of his neck told a different story. The way it prickled, he knew he was being watched.

The bar was on the left. Tables were scattered through the middle of the room. On the right-hand wall were curtained booths for privacy. In the back was an open area where a very attractive young woman in a low-cut white blouse and long, colorful skirt was dancing to the accompaniment of three men with guitars. Her slipper-shod feet moved with blinding speed on the stone floor. Some of the men drinking at the tables clapped along with the music and called encouragement to her.

The cantina was busy with only a few open spaces at the bar. The tables were all full. Braddock turned toward the bar but, before he could take a step, someone moved

51

up beside him on the right. Since that was his gun arm, the person's presence made warning bells go off in Braddock's brain. He moved his hand toward the holstered Colt.

Then, he saw that the person who had come up to him was a young woman, equally as beautiful as the dancer if not more so. She smiled and put a hand on his sleeve. He pulled his arm back, not wanting her to slow his draw if he needed to make one.

"Take it easy, señor," she said in good English. "Do I look like I mean you any harm?"

"Bad things sometimes come in pretty packages," Braddock said.

She certainly qualified on the second part of that, he thought. Smooth skin just darker than honey and plenty of it on display in the blouse that left her shoulders and the upper swells of her breasts in view. Waves of rich brown hair that tumbled around her face. Shadowy eyes with devils dancing in them. Once again, she rested a hand with long, crimson fingernails on his arm.

"How can you look at me," she asked, "and think that I am bad?"

"What's your name?" Braddock asked instead of answering.

"Elena."

At first glance, he had thought she was very young, maybe fifteen or sixteen. Now, he saw that she was older than that, more like nineteen or twenty. The lines around her eyes and mouth were very faint but they were there, testifying that her life had not been an easy one.

"What is it you want with me, Elena?"

She inclined her head toward one of the curtained booths and said, "Come sit with me. We will drink, talk, laugh...I don't think you have laughed enough in your life, señor."

It had been a while since Braddock had seen a lot to laugh about, that was true enough. But as he slowly nodded, he wasn't agreeing with the girl because of that. According to Rainey, Manuel Santiago spent most of his time in Alamoros and this appeared to be the largest, busiest cantina. He had sought it out for the same reason he had gone into the Palomino Saloon in Cemetery Butte that morning. There was information to be had in such places.

There was information to be gotten from young women like Elena. She might even be able to tell him where to find Manuel Santiago.

"All right," Braddock said. "You want to get a bottle and some glasses from the bartender?"

"They await us already, señor."

She moved to link her left arm with his right but he stopped her and said, "Come around on this other side."

"You gringos. Always so suspicious."

"I like to think of it as being careful."

The air smelled of tequila, cerveza, tobacco, hemp, and human flesh. Even with that potent mix in his nostrils, Braddock caught the scent of flowers from Elena's hair. For a second, it made him remember a girl named Rosaria...but she was gone and thinking about her wouldn't do anybody any good.

As they neared the booth, a burly, bearded man in sombrero and serape stood up from the table where he had been drinking with friends. He turned toward the entrance, and the way he swayed on his feet showed how drunk he was.

Or how drunk he was pretending to be. Braddock kept an eye on the man and when he lurched toward

Braddock, the Ranger was ready. He twisted out of the way of a potential knife thrust and took Elena with him.

The drunken vaquero banged his shoulder against Braddock's, though, then took an unsteady step back and cursed. His breath was so laden with tequila, Braddock thought that if he lit a match, flames would erupt from the man's mouth like he was a dragon.

"Paco, no—" Elena began.

The drunken man cursed her as well as Braddock and swung a big fist at the Texan's head.

If Paco was putting on an act, he was doing a mighty fine job of it. The punch was slow and lumbering and Braddock had no trouble getting out of its way. The miss threw Paco even more off-balance than he already was. Braddock caught his wrist, twisted his arm behind his back.

"Ah, dios mio!" Paco gasped.

Braddock glanced around. A few people in the room were watching the confrontation, including Paco's friends at the nearby table. The girl in the back of the room was still dancing, though, and the musicians hadn't missed a beat. From the lack of reaction, Braddock figured that Paco getting drunk and trying to start a fight wasn't an unusual occurrence. Maybe this little fracas was harmless after all.

Braddock leaned close to Paco's ear and asked in Spanish if the man spoke English.

"Sí, a little," Paco replied in a strained voice.

"I'm not looking for trouble, amigo. I'm sorry I bumped into you." Braddock put a little pressure on Paco's arm, enough so that the man could tell it wouldn't be any trouble for Braddock to pop it out of its socket. "All right?"

"S-sí," Paco said. "I...I accept your apology, señor."

"Good. I'd just as soon be friends." Braddock let go of Paco's arm and stepped back. He took a coin from his pocket and pressed it into the big man's hand. "Buy your friends a drink on me."

"Sí, señor. Muchas gracias." Paco nodded toward the door. "As soon as I get back. I've had a *lot* to drink tonight already."

Braddock smiled and said, "I can tell."

Paco stumbled on toward the batwings and went out into the night. Whether he would come back and spend that dinero on his friends or keep it all for himself, Braddock didn't know or care.

"Thank you, Señor Braddock," Elena said quietly beside him. "Paco means no harm. He is like a big shaggy dog who doesn't know his own strength." She linked arms with Braddock again and urged him the last few steps to the booth. "Besides, I did not want a fight drawing attention to us."

That statement was enough to give Braddock pause. If she was just one of the girls who worked in this cantina, why would she care if anyone paid attention to her doing her job?

That was really just an afterthought, though, because she had said something else that caused alarm to shoot through him. He stopped and said, "I never told you my name and I've never been in this town before."

Something sharp prodded against his left side. Never losing the smile on her face, Elena said, "This knife is sharp enough to slide right between your ribs and into your heart with just a little push, señor. No matter how fast you are with your gun, I can kill you before you kill me."

"How about neither one of us dies?" Braddock suggested. "What is it you want from me?"

"Sit down in the booth. Someone wants to talk to you."

Well, thought Braddock, he had come in here in hopes of learning something. Maybe this was one way to do it.

He stepped up to the booth and moved the curtain aside.

A man sat there waiting tensely in the shadows.

9

"THANK GOD," CHARLES HORNER SAID. "I WAS WATCHING through the gap in the curtains and I thought there was going to be a...a shootout."

As usual, Braddock tried not to let surprise show on his tanned features but the bespectacled secretary from Massachusetts was just about the last hombre he'd expected to run into in this cantina.

"Please sit down," Horner went on. "I really need to talk to you, Ranger Braddock."

"Why don't you start by not calling me that?" Braddock said as he slid onto the bench across from Horner. "That is, if you really don't want to attract attention."

The man took a folded handkerchief from his shirt pocket and patted away beads of sweat from his forehead. It was hot and stuffy inside the cantina but Braddock didn't think that was the only reason Horner was sweating.

"I don't," Horner said. He slid over on the bench to make room for Elena, who sat down and pulled the curtains so that only a tiny gap remained between them.

A candle burned in the center of the table. Beside it was a bottle of tequila and an empty glass. Horner had an empty glass in front of him, too, but Braddock could see a little liquor clinging to the inside of it. The secretary had gotten a head start.

"Please, help yourself to a drink," Horner said as he gestured at the bottle.

Braddock nodded toward Elena and asked, "What about the lady?"

She laughed softly and said, "I don't drink."

Instead, she took a quirley from a pocket hidden somewhere in her voluminous skirt, put one end between her lips, and leaned forward to puff it into life as she held the tip in the candle flame. The odor of burning hemp filled the booth as she blew out some smoke.

Braddock poured a couple of fingers of tequila in the empty glass, sipped the fiery stuff. He said bluntly, "What the hell are you doing here, Horner?"

"I followed Jason down here, after I saw him arguing with Jack Conover."

"Did you happen to overhear what they were fighting about?" Braddock asked.

"Not really but I did catch a few words. I heard Conover say something about...about mules. He wasn't happy. Then Jason told him to be patient."

Braddock took another sip of tequila and nodded slowly. What Horner was telling him fit in with a vague theory that had started to form in Braddock's brain while he was riding down here. It was prompted by memories of the bitterness he had heard in Jason Rainey's voice when Jason was explaining how his mother had died after being dragged from one primitive frontier outpost to another by his father.

That was enough to make Jason blame Rainey for his mother's death and that could have caused resentment. Resentment often led to hate.

Enough hate to make Jason strike back against his father by planning that ambush in Buzzard's Canyon?

Happy Jack Conover was capable of taking part in such a massacre, Braddock thought. Some of the other men on Rainey's crew probably were, too. Maybe Rainey had hired them to rustle Felipe Santiago's cattle and force Santiago into selling his share of the mine cheaply. But even if that was true, Conover and the others could have double-crossed Rainey later on when Jason offered them a share of the gold.

It made sense but Braddock had no proof.

Maybe he could find some while Jason was down here below the border. Maybe Jason would lead him right to where the gold was stashed...

"Where's Jason now?" Braddock asked.

"You're thinking what I'm thinking, aren't you?" Horner said in return. "That Jason was responsible somehow for what happened?"

Horner sounded miserable. He probably didn't want to believe it was possible for a son to turn on his father so completely. Braddock could believe it, though. He had seen such things, and worse, during his time as a Ranger.

"It seems like it could have happened that way," Braddock said slowly.

Horner blotted sweat from his forehead again and nodded.

"I know. That's why I followed him. I...I felt like I needed to be certain."

"You didn't tell me where he is," Braddock pointed out.

It was Elena who answered. She took a drag on the

quirley, held it for a second, and then said, "He's in one of the rooms in the back, with a girl."

Braddock looked at her with narrowed eyes and asked, "What's your part in this?"

"I have no part," she said. "Carlos and I are friends, that's all."

It took a second for Braddock to realize she was talking about Charles Horner. He said, "Really?"

His obvious skepticism caused Horner to flush and look down at the table in embarrassment but Elena's eyes flashed with anger.

"He is a very intelligent man," she said. "He has many good qualities."

"I'm sure he does."

"I'm sitting right here, you know," Horner muttered.

"Sorry, Charles," Braddock said. "No offense. You just don't seem like the sort to go adventuring south of the border. How'd you get down here, anyway?"

"I brought a buggy. And as for why I came, I don't want Mr. Rainey to be hurt any more than he already has been." Horner paused. "Unfortunately, that may be unavoidable."

"If his son turns out to be a murderer and a gold thief, you mean."

Horner looked down at the table again and sighed.

"It's liable to kill him. But if Jason is responsible for this, he can't be allowed to get away with it. For one thing, what will he do next?"

That was a good question, Braddock thought. If Jason Rainey was the mastermind, the next move he made against his father might be even worse.

Braddock wasn't ready to accept that theory completely just yet, though. He said, "What about

Manuel Santiago? He's got a grudge against Rainey, too. Maybe he's to blame for the ambush." Something else occurred to him. "Or maybe he and Jason are working together, Jason to avenge his mother and Manuel to settle the score for his father."

"No," Elena said flatly. "That isn't possible. Manuel Santiago is dead."

Braddock leaned back against the bench and said, "You're sure about that?"

"I am certain, Señor Braddock. I knew Manuel. He is gone."

"How did he die?"

"Foolishly."

Clearly, she didn't want to say anything more about the subject. Braddock was willing to let it go for now because he wanted to concentrate on Jason Rainey. He needed proof that Jason was involved in the massacre.

Once he had that, if it existed, then he could indulge his curiosity and find out more about what had happened to Manuel Santiago.

"What are you going to do now?" Horner asked.

"You say Jason's in the back with a girl?"

Elena nodded and said, "Sí. Her name is Amelia."

"What will he do when he's finished?"

"He usually leaves through the back door."

"Then if I wait back there, I can follow him, see where he goes," Braddock mused.

"He might just go back to the ranch," Horner said doubtfully.

"Why would he come all the way down here just to be with a whore? He could have done that at the Palomino or one of the other saloons in Cemetery Butte. Unless she's one special whore...?"

Elena shook her head and said, "He has no favorites. I've been with him myself, several times."

She appeared not to notice how Horner winced a little at that casual comment.

"Then he just stopped here before he goes on to his real reason for crossing the border," Braddock said. "I want to find out what that is."

"Then I guess it's a good idea for you to follow him," Horner said. "Do you want me to come with you?"

Braddock shook his head. Jason might lead him straight into trouble and the last thing he wanted was to be saddled with looking after this Easterner.

"No, you go on back to the ranch." Braddock smiled faintly. "Or stay here and visit with Elena. Doesn't matter to me."

"I will show you where Jason will come out," she said. "Get your horse and go around back. I'll meet you. But first I will make sure that Jason is still busy."

"Good idea. I don't want to bump into him."

Elena took one more deep drag on the smoke as Braddock parted the curtains and slid out of the booth.

A different girl was dancing to the guitar music now. She wasn't as pretty as the first one but her slim brown legs moved just as swiftly and deftly under the billowing skirt.

Braddock stepped outside and untied the dun from the hitch rail. Other than the cantina, Alamoros was quiet now. Most people were settling down for the night.

But he was just getting started, Braddock thought.

He led the horse around the big adobe building. When he reached the back, he saw that there was a barn and a corral not far away. The barn might make a good place for him to wait for Jason Rainey.

Elena stepped out of the shadows next to the cantina's rear wall. She came toward Braddock and whispered, "Jason is still inside with Amelia. But I think he will be leaving soon. You can hide in the barn."

"I was just thinking the same thing," Braddock told her.

He led the dun to the big double doors. One side was open a foot or so. Braddock grasped the door and pulled it back wide enough for him to take the horse inside.

Thick shadows closed in around them. Braddock could barely see Elena as she stepped into the barn and moved beside him.

"You don't have to stay out here," he said. "Be better if you go back inside."

"I don't mind staying." She put her hand on Braddock's arm as she had done a couple of times already this evening. He smelled the scent of flowers again, although this time it was mixed with the hemp she'd been smoking.

"Not a good idea," he said. "I've got to keep an eye out for Jason."

"I'll know when he's leaving."

Somewhere behind Braddock, a horse stamped and blew. That was nothing unusual in a barn but it prompted him to glance over his shoulder anyway.

By now, his eyes had adjusted enough to the darkness that he was able to spot the shape of a buggy parked in the barn's center aisle with a couple of horses still hitched to it.

Like fireworks going off on the Fourth of July, connections suddenly popped in Braddock's brain. The buggy back here, the horse with the Spade brand tied out front, Jason Rainey supposedly coming out soon from the cantina's rear door...

Something just wasn't right.

Elena must have felt him tense and realized that he'd figured out she was lying to him. As Braddock started to pull away from her and reach for his gun, she cried, "Now, Paco!"

10

PACO HAD EITHER SOBERED UP IN A HURRY OR HE WAS A
better actor than Braddock had given him credit for.
There was nothing clumsy or lumbering about his
movements as he lunged out from behind the buggy and
tackled Braddock.

The impact was enough to drive Braddock off his
feet. He landed on the hard-packed dirt with Paco on top
of him. That drove all the air out of Braddock's lungs
and left him momentarily stunned. Paco hammered
punches around Braddock's head and shoulders.

Survival instinct made Braddock arch his back and
buck upward from the ground. Paco tried to hang on by
clamping his knees around Braddock's torso but Braddock reacted too fast and his wiry strength was too
much. Paco toppled off of him.

Gasping for breath, Braddock rolled over and pushed
up to his hands and knees. He sensed as much as heard
something coming through the air toward him and
threw himself to the side. Something thudded into the

ground and Elena said, "Ooof!" Braddock knew she had just tried to hit him with a club of some sort.

He didn't know if she wanted him dead or was trying to knock him unconscious and, at the moment, it didn't really matter. It seemed, though, that if she just wanted to kill him she could have done it before now.

He couldn't rely on her wanting him alive. He rolled fast across the floor, crashed into her legs, and reached up to grab her skirt and pull her down. She sprawled on top of him.

There was a time when Braddock would have had compunctions about hitting a woman but no longer. He swung a backhand and felt it crack against her head. She cried out and fell away from him. He scrambled up but had just gotten to his feet when what felt like a piledriver slammed into his belly. He doubled over, almost passing out from the shock and pain, then fell to his knees.

Paco loomed over him, holding up the bludgeon Elena had wielded a few minutes earlier.

"You want me to bust his head open?" he asked her.

"No," she said. "I want him to live for now."

Braddock looked up, saw Paco shrug. He knew he needed to get up and fight but, no matter how hard he tried, he couldn't get his muscles to obey him.

A second later, Paco's boot connected with Braddock's skull in a vicious kick and Braddock went over backward.

He was out cold when he hit the ground and never felt it.

WHEN HE WOKE, he was sick from being knocked out and the rocking motion didn't help. He started to retch. Somewhere nearby, Elena called, "Paco!"

A moment later, strong hands took hold of Braddock, hauled him out of wherever he was, and dumped him on the ground as he heaved up everything in his belly. It didn't amount to much, thankfully, because he hadn't eaten since the noonday meal at Martin Rainey's ranch house.

"Get him up," Elena ordered coldly.

Paco's big hands closed roughly on Braddock and lifted him. Braddock's legs were useless at the moment. He would have collapsed if Paco hadn't held him up.

He blinked bleary eyes and managed to focus them on the buggy, which was visible in the moonlight as it sat motionless at the edge of a trail. Rugged peaks and ridges dotted with trees and brush loomed around them.

Charles Horner sat in the buggy holding the reins. Elena was beside him. She had a rifle across her knees. Braddock's dun was tied to the back of the vehicle and another saddle horse that was bound to be Paco's stood nearby, its reins dangling.

"Now that he's awake, tie his hands behind him," Elena told Paco. "Then throw him behind the seat again."

In an irritated voice, Horner said, "I don't see why we're going to this much trouble. It would have been easier just to kill him, dump his body in the hills, and let the coyotes have him."

Even though Braddock still felt sick and dizzy, a bleak smile stretched across his face.

"That's mighty cold-blooded talk for a secretary," he said.

Horner blew out a disgusted breath and said, "I'm hardly just a secretary, Ranger Braddock. I'm the man who's going to destroy Martin Rainey for what he's done."

Braddock forced his brain to work despite the fuzziness he felt. He remembered what had been said at the meal he'd shared with Rainey and Horner, and he said, "This is about your father."

"It was Rainey's vainglorious foolishness that got him killed," Horner snapped. "He was an ambitious man. He was going to be a general, to hear him tell it, so he took stupid risks no commanding officer should have. He led his men into an Apache ambush and got three-fourths of them killed, including his adjutant, my father, who died saving that bastard's life. That was the end of his military career, even if his wife hadn't died." Horner paused. "I wish she had suffered more, so maybe he would have, too."

"You set up the ambush of that mule train," Braddock accused. "Who bossed it? Conover?"

"I thought you might have recognized him. Yes, he was in charge of it. He and a man named Scanlon were the ones who tried to kill you in the canyon this afternoon. Scanlon was the wrangler who took Jason's horse when the two of you rode in this morning. He didn't make it out of the canyon."

"You pushed that rock down on him so I wouldn't recognize him and go back to Rainey's headquarters." Braddock shook his head. "I wouldn't have thought you had that in you, either, Horner."

Elena said, "I told you, Carlos is a man of many unexpected abilities." She sounded impatient as she added, "But we've talked enough. I want to get to the mine."

"Of course, my dear," Horner said. "Paco?"

The big man lashed Braddock's wrists together with rawhide thongs, marched him over to the buggy, and half-shoved, half-threw him into the narrow space behind the seat. That made Braddock's head spin crazily again for several seconds.

Horner got the team moving again. The buggy bumped and swayed over the trail. Elena had said they were going to the mine and there was only one place she could have meant, despite the fact that the statement didn't really make sense to Braddock.

The way he was lying on the buggy's hard floorboard, he was really uncomfortable, so he tried to distract himself from that by saying, "Was Jason Rainey really in Alamoros tonight?"

"He was there," Horner said without looking around. "That part of what I told you was true. He was with that girl Amelia, too. Elena told her to keep him busy until we managed to get you outside. He was the bait we used to catch you."

"But if he didn't have anything to do with ambushing the mule train, why was he there?"

Elena laughed and said, "Because he likes putas, why else? Jason would be content to spend the rest of his life drinking and whoring and feeling sorry for himself because his mother is dead."

"You sound like you know him pretty well," Braddock said as another idea tickled the back of his mind. With the shape he was in, plus the fact that he was tied up securely, there really wasn't anything he could do right now to turn this situation around but it wouldn't hurt to learn as much of the truth as he could.

"I know him too well," Elena said. "I hate him. I hate his cruelty, the way he takes advantage of people—"

She stopped short as if she didn't want to say too much.

"Horner, what about the rustling?" Braddock asked.

"You mean when the cattle were stolen from Don Felipe Santiago's ranch?" Horner said. "What about it?"

"Was Martin Rainey behind it? Did Conover ramrod that job, too?"

"You know, I'm honestly not sure," Horner said. "I tried to find out but I never could. It wouldn't surprise me a bit, though, knowing Rainey the way I do. The man's ruthless. But whether he did or not, he still took advantage of Don Felipe. It just wasn't right, how he made Don Felipe take a fraction of what his share of the mine was worth. A mere pittance. If Rainey had treated him fairly, he might have had a chance to hold on to his ranch."

"You know a lot about that, don't you?" Braddock said. "Who told you? Elena?"

She turned in the seat to glare down at him and say, "Shut up! I'll take this rifle and smash your teeth in with the butt if you keep talking."

Braddock ignored the threat and went on, "You're Santiago's daughter, aren't you, Elena? Rainey mentioned that Manuel had a sister but I'd forgotten about that until just now. Looks like Rainey had the wrong sibling pegged as the one who wants revenge."

"I'm warning you, Ranger—"

"You and Horner wanted the same thing," Braddock interrupted her. "To ruin Martin Rainey and make him suffer. So you threw in together."

"That's right," Elena said. "And before the night is over, he's going to die, he and that dog of a son."

"Why move so fast? You just started your grand plan, didn't you? Killing all those men and stealing that gold, that was just the first step."

"We don't have the luxury of taking our time anymore," Horner said. "You ought to know that, Braddock. Now that the Rangers are involved, we have to go ahead and kill Rainey and Jason, take our share of the gold, and disappear forever in Mexico. It would have been nice to make Rainey suffer longer but I can be satisfied with sending the son of a bitch to hell where he belongs."

Braddock let his head sag back and laughed. He couldn't help it. They had no way of knowing that he was an outlaw Ranger, not the real thing anymore. Captain Hughes would have heard about the massacre in Buzzard's Canyon and eventually he might send a man out here to investigate it but, as short-handed as the Rangers were, it was just as likely that they would never take an official interest in the case.

But Horner and Elena didn't know that. They didn't have a clue.

They wanted to kill him to prevent something that probably would never happen anyway.

"He's gone loco," Elena said. "But he'll stop laughing soon enough. We're here."

The buggy lurched to a halt. Paco dismounted, reached into the vehicle, dragged Braddock out, and stood him up. In the moonlight, Braddock saw several buildings scattered around, and beyond them, like a yawning black mouth, an opening in the mountainside with several wagons parked near it.

"This is your new home, Ranger," Elena said. "Welcome to hell."

11

"THIS IS RAINEY'S MINE?" BRADDOCK ASKED.

"This is my father's mine!" Elena snapped. "It was his dream. He made it happen. And then Rainey stole it from him!" She tossed her head defiantly, making the thick waves of dark hair stir around her face. "Now, I have stolen it back."

Several men emerged from one of the buildings and walked toward them in the moonlight. They carried rifles and, even though Braddock didn't recognize them, he knew the type. Hardcases, hired killers, the sort of men who would do any job, no matter how brutal, if the pay was right.

Including butchering a bunch of innocent men, as they had done in Buzzard's Canyon.

"Your men moved in here at the mine, killed the guards who were loyal to Rainey, and took over," Braddock said. "Is that about the size of it?"

"That's right," Elena said from the buggy seat.

"Why not just do that to start with? Why murder all those men with the mule train?"

"Because I wanted their blood on Rainey's hands! I wanted him to suffer from the guilt he would feel over their deaths."

Charles Horner said, "That's one area in which we disagreed. I told Elena that Martin Rainey wasn't capable of feeling any guilt because he never believes that he's in the wrong. That's just not something that's a part of him."

"We've been working the men here as hard as we can, to take out as much gold as possible," Elena went on. "We'll keep doing that even after Rainey is dead, for a while, anyway. Maybe from now on. With Rainey and Jason gone, who's going to stop us?"

"You were afraid the Rangers might," Braddock reminded her. "That's why you moved up your timetable."

Elena scoffed.

"We're too far across the border," she said. "The Rangers won't come all this way."

She might be wrong about that, thought Braddock, but it didn't matter since the Rangers weren't really mixed up in this.

Horner said, "That's one reason I'm a little worried about snatching Braddock like this. When the Rangers realize he's disappeared, won't they come looking for him?"

"They'll search on the other side of the Rio Grande first," Elena said confidently. "Anyway, we're going to keep him alive. He can work in the mine and we can use him as a hostage if we need to."

Braddock smiled a little. He wouldn't be much good to them as a hostage. The Rangers wanted to arrest him, that was all. Other than that, they didn't care if he lived or died.

"Dios mio, you people like to prattle on," Elena continued. "Paco, take Braddock into the mine and put him with the others."

"Sí, querida," Paco said.

Elena made a disgusted sound in response to the endearment but Paco either didn't hear her or chose to ignore it. He shoved Braddock toward the black mouth of the mine tunnel. A couple of the men carrying rifles fell in behind them.

As Braddock came closer to the mine, he saw a red glow flickering deep in the darkness. *Welcome to hell*, Elena had said, and that was what this looked like, Braddock realized: the gateway to Hades itself.

Braddock looked over his shoulder and asked, "Were you really drunk back there in Alamoros, Paco, or were you just taking Elena's orders?"

The big man chuckled and said, "I was drunk, all right, señor, but not as drunk as you thought. I was supposed to start a fight with you and knock you out, so we could bring you here without involving Señor Horner. But that failed."

"You sound like you're a pretty smart hombre. You know that Elena and Horner are both crazy, don't you? They'll do anything to get their revenge and they don't care who else gets hurt. Hell, earlier today Horner dropped a damn boulder on a man who might've still been alive. A man who worked for him...like you do."

"I work for Señorita Santiago," Paco said. "And trying to turn me against her will do you no good, Ranger. You should save your breath." He laughed again. "You'll need it."

Braddock fell silent. He had to see what awaited him inside the mine before he could make any more plans.

That didn't take long. Paco prodded him into the

tunnel. The red glow grew stronger as they delved deeper into the mountainside. The tunnel bent to the right and, around the turn, the passage opened up into a large, high-ceilinged chamber with a tunnel continuing deeper into the mine on the far side. The chamber was lit by several lanterns. One part of the room was separated from the rest by a wall of iron bars set into the stone ceiling and floor.

That made Braddock frown in puzzlement. Those bars had been there for a while, since before the gunmen working for Horner and Elena had taken over the mine. Why were they there? Had Martin Rainey been keeping his workers locked up here like slaves?

There were men on the wrong side of those bars now, more than a dozen prisoners crowded into the closed-off area. They wore what had once been the white, pajama-like outfit of farmers, although now the garments were so stained and dirty they were almost black.

Except for one man whose clothing was better, although still considerably worn, stained, and ragged. He looked like he had been a vaquero at one time. Now he was as haggard and exhausted as his fellow prisoners.

On the other side of the room were bunks and tables, as well as quite a few crates stacked up against the wall. Four men sat at one of the tables playing cards and passing around a bottle of tequila. They had shotguns within easy reach and they forgot about their game and stood up as Braddock, Paco, and the other two men came into the chamber. They were guards, Braddock knew, more members of the gang Elena and Horner had put together.

"Who's this?" one of the men asked as he frowned at Braddock. "Somebody else to dig?"

"This is a Texas Ranger," Paco said with a big grin. "His name is Braddock. But now, he is one of the nameless ones who exist only to labor and make us rich."

The guards smirked. They were hardcases, the sort of men Braddock had chased down and arrested or killed when he was a real lawman. They would enjoy making life a living hell for him down here under the ground.

One of the guards said, "Cut him loose and we'll put him in there." They picked up their shotguns and covered Braddock as Paco stepped behind him and drew a Bowie knife from a fringed sheath at his waist. The men with the rifles moved back, out of the line of fire for the scatterguns.

"Aren't you afraid I'll try something and you'll get cut down, too?" Braddock asked Paco.

"You're between me and the shotguns, Señor Ranger," Paco said. "True, I'm bigger than you and might catch a little of the buckshot but you would stop most of it, especially at this range. I'd still have a good chance to live. You, none at all."

He was right about that, Braddock thought. The odds were too high right now for him to make a play.

But if he allowed them to lock him up in there, would he ever have another chance?

As Paco used the Bowie to saw on the tough rawhide thongs, Braddock said, "Why is there a prison in here? Did Rainey keep his workers locked up like this? Doesn't seem right."

"Señor Rainey is a bad man but, no, he didn't lock up his miners. That area was used for storage, to keep the dynamite and the other supplies locked up." Paco laughed. "There are many bandits in Mexico, you know."

Braddock's gaze darted toward the crates stacked against the other wall. They must have been moved out of the storage area. Some of them had dynamite in them, he thought, and that gave him an idea.

The prisoner who looked like a vaquero came to the bars and gripped them. His lean, dark face was angry as he said, "You cannot do this, Paco. You were once a good man, an honest man, a hard worker."

Paco looked over Braddock's shoulder and said, "And what did that ever get me, eh? Enough money for a bottle of pulqué and a whore once a month."

"My father took better care of you than that and you know it," the young man shot back at him. "He would not want you doing this."

"What? Following your sister's orders? Helping to avenge his death, the way you were too weak to do?"

Braddock drew in a sharp breath. He realized he was looking at Manuel Santiago. Elena had claimed that her brother was dead. Obviously, she hadn't meant that literally. They must have had a falling out over Elena's desire for revenge on Martin Rainey and Manuel had wound up being locked away and enslaved by his own sister.

Manuel was dead to Elena, Braddock supposed. That was what she had meant.

She really was loco, he thought.

And she and Horner planned to return to Rainey's ranch tonight to murder him and Jason. For all Braddock knew, they were already gone, heading north again toward the Rio Grande. Because of that, he couldn't afford to bide his time, no matter how bad the odds were against him.

The last of the rawhide thongs fell away from Braddock's wrists. One of the guards lowered his shotgun and stepped to the door set into the bars. He took a key from where it hung on his belt. The other three guards swung around and pointed their shotguns toward

Manuel Santiago and the rest of the prisoners, forcing them to move away from the bars and the door.

Braddock figured the two men from outside still had him covered with their rifles but at least the Greeners weren't aimed at him now. This was the best chance he was going to get.

By now he had recovered from being knocked out. His mind was clear and his muscles were working smoothly. He stumbled anyway as Paco pushed him toward the cell. The man at the door unlocked it and swung it open.

"Get in—" the big man began.

Braddock twisted and lunged, ramming his shoulder into Paco's chest and driving him backward. The move took Paco by surprise. His feet weren't braced. He swayed back just as one of the riflemen pulled the trigger. The bullet smacked into Paco's shoulder and made him howl in pain as echoes from the shot racketed back and forth inside the chamber.

Braddock left his feet in a leaping dive. He wasn't going after any of the guards, though. Instead, his hand closed around the bale attached to one of the lanterns sitting on a table. He rolled over as another shot blasted. With a whip-like motion of his arm, he flung the lantern at the stack of crates on the far wall.

The glass reservoir shattered as it hit them, and flame exploded from the spraying kerosene.

"The dynamite!" one of the guards shouted in shrill panic. "The dynamite!"

THE TWO RIFLEMEN TURNED AND DASHED FOR THE MOUTH of the tunnel. So did one of the shotgunners.

Some of the men behind the bars cried out in fear but others, including Manuel Santiago, stampeded toward the open door. The guard who had just unlocked it tried to slam it closed again but Manuel leaped forward and struck the door with his shoulder, knocking it back against the guard and staggering him.

In a continuation of the same movement that had sent the lantern flying across the chamber, Braddock rolled over again just as a guard triggered both barrels of his scattergun. The double load of buckshot slammed into the floor, barely missing Braddock.

Paco staggered back and forth, yelling as he clutched his wounded shoulder with his other hand. He steadied himself, focused his rage on Braddock, and charged just as the outlaw Ranger surged to his feet.

Braddock saw Paco barreling toward him like a runaway freight train and knew that if the big man was able to catch him in a bear hug, Paco might well crush the life out of him. That knowledge gave Braddock the desperate speed he needed to twist out of the way. He clubbed his hands together and smashed them against the back of Paco's neck as the man went past him. That blow drove Paco face first into the bars.

Manuel Santiago grabbed the twin barrels of the guard's shotgun and wrenched them upward. The man let go of the weapon and clawed at the revolver on his hip instead, but, before he could draw it, Manuel rammed the shotgun's butt into his throat. The man staggered, gagging and gasping as he tried to draw air through his shattered windpipe.

He didn't have to struggle for breath for long because, a second later, Manuel cracked his skull with a second stroke.

A few feet away, the other prisoners poured out of the makeshift cell, still yelling and screaming and practically trampling on each other as they tried to get out of the mine before the dynamite exploded. They stomped right over the guard who was trying to reload his shotgun. His cries lasted only a moment.

Meanwhile, on the other side of the chamber, the flames leaped higher as several of the crates burned. The fire spread to the cots and they began to blaze as well.

Paco bounced off the bars and tried to wheel around toward Braddock but he ran right into another blow from the clubbed fists. This one landed on Paco's already broken and bleeding nose. Paco hit the bars again, this time with his back, and, when he rebounded, he pitched forward and landed face down. He didn't get up.

Braddock leaned down and pulled Paco's Colt from its holster, then scooped the big man's fallen Bowie knife from the floor. He turned to Manuel Santiago, who was the only one left in the chamber who was still conscious.

The rest of the prisoners had fled around the bend in the tunnel.

"We'd better get out of here," Braddock said. "There's a good chance that dynamite won't explode but it still might."

Manuel grinned and said, "I knew burning wouldn't set it off. I grew up around this mine."

"Some of those other fellas probably know that, too, if they'd stop to think about it," Braddock said dryly. "Good thing they didn't."

As they trotted around the bend, more shots blasted, but these came from outside. Up ahead, men shouted and cried out in pain. The workers came flooding back along the tunnel.

"The guards got out!" one of the men told Manuel. "Now they and the others shoot at us! They won't let us out! We're going to die!"

"Not yet," Braddock said. He stuffed Paco's gun in the waistband of his trousers and turned to run back to the chamber. The hellish glare was even brighter now, since the fire was bigger.

Braddock put a hand in front of his face to shield it a little from the heat as he approached the inferno. One of the crates hadn't caught fire yet. He bent and grabbed it, jerked it up and turned to run along the tunnel. He knew how nitroglycerine sometimes sweated out of dynamite and pooled in the bottom of a crate like this, creating a bomb that took only a little jostling to set it off. He could only hope that hadn't happened with the dynamite in this crate.

If it had, he'd never know it. One second he'd be here, the next blasted to kingdom come.

Nothing happened.

The miners had retreated from the entrance. Bullets

from outside still came through the opening and whined off the tunnel walls. The men huddled behind whatever cover they could find, caught between ruthless killers in front of them and what they feared was about to be a huge explosion behind them.

Manuel Santiago was crouched behind a small outcropping of rock. Braddock set the crate down beside him. Manuel's eyes got a little bigger as he looked at it.

"Fire might not set that off, but if a bullet were to hit one of the sticks—"

"Don't reckon you've got any blasting caps and fuses," Braddock said.

"They'd be back there with the supplies. The ones you set on fire."

Braddock used the Bowie knife to pry the top off the crate. He was going to feel damned foolish, he thought, if he found that it was full of, say, canned peaches instead of high explosives.

He knew from the acrid smell of the contents that it was dynamite. He reached in and pulled one of the red, paper-wrapped cylinders from its packing.

"Give me one of those shotgun shells," he said to Manuel.

"What are you going to do? Whatever it is, I think you must be insane."

Braddock started digging around in the end of the dynamite with the knife point to hollow it out. Manuel edged away from him, eyes growing even bigger in the tunnel's gloom.

"The shell," Braddock said again.

Manuel broke open the shotgun and drew the unfired shell out of the right-hand barrel. He gave it to Braddock, who wedged the end of it into the hole he'd gouged in the dynamite.

"That'll work for a blasting cap," Braddock said.

"How are you going to set it off?"

"Figure if I can hit the end of the shell with a bullet, that'll do the trick."

"Like I said, loco!" Manuel exclaimed. "No one could make a shot like that."

"Well, if I don't, we may not get out of here alive," Braddock said. "That doesn't leave me much choice except to make it, does it?"

Manuel just stared at him.

Braddock used the Bowie's handle to hammer down the lid on the crate. He put the stick of dynamite in his pocket and picked up the crate, then edged along the wall toward the entrance.

Manuel came up behind him and said, "You may be loco, Ranger, but you're our best chance of getting out of here, I suppose. Can I help you?"

Braddock took the Colt from his waistband and handed it to the young man.

"I'm liable to need some covering fire. Let's see if we can tell where those guards are holed up."

Muzzles flashes that bloomed like crimson flowers in the darkness gave Braddock his answer as he edged forward for a look. The guards had taken cover behind the three ore wagons parked about forty feet from the tunnel mouth. They kept up a sporadic attack, shooting now and then at the opening in the slope.

Braddock drew back, told Manuel what he had seen, then asked, "How many rounds in that gun?"

Manuel opened the cylinder to check.

"Five," he reported.

"All right. You're going to fire three shots, one at each wagon, as fast as you can. That'll make them duck and give me time to heave this crate and toss the stick I rigged. Then I'll have two bullets left to try to hit that shotgun shell."

"And if you can't?" Manuel asked, his voice grim.

"At least we tried," Braddock said.

Manuel sighed and hefted the Colt. He nodded.

"Whenever you are ready, Ranger."

Braddock waited until a flurry of shots came from outside, then snapped, "Now."

Manuel sprang into the opening and started shooting. Braddock dashed up beside him, swung the crate over his head, and threw it toward the wagons as hard as he could. Men yelled in alarm when they saw it coming. The crate landed in front of the middle wagon and broke open, scattering some of the dynamite. Most of it stayed in a heap inside the busted crate.

Before the crate ever landed, Braddock snatched the rigged-up stick from his pocket. He threw it end over end. It hit, bounced, and came to rest less than a foot from what was left of the crate.

Braddock and Manuel darted back into the tunnel as the gunmen opened up again. Bullets whined around them.

"All right, let me have the Colt," Braddock said over the racket.

"This is madness," Manuel muttered. "Sheer madness."

Outside, one of the men yelled, "Damn it, somebody get that dynamite!"

"You get it!" another man responded. "I'm not goin' anywhere near the damn stuff!"

Braddock crawled back to the opening, stretched out on his belly, and propped himself on his elbows. He used both hands to steady the Colt as he drew back the hammer. The moonlight washing over the scene wasn't as bright as day but he could see what he was shooting at.

He took a deep breath, held it, and squeezed the trigger.

The Colt roared and bucked in his hands. The bullet struck a few inches shy of the target.

"Son of a bitch!" one of the gunmen bellowed. "I'm not gettin' paid enough to get blowed up!"

"Neither am I!" another man agreed. "Let's get outta here!"

Several forms leaped from the cover of the wagons and raced toward the corral where horses milled. Another man fired a couple of wild shots at the tunnel, then fled as well. Braddock couldn't tell how many men were left behind but one of them cursed bitterly. His voice shook and Braddock knew his nerve was breaking.

Hoofbeats pounded in the night. The men who had fled were galloping away bareback, not even taking the time to saddle their mounts.

Manuel had crawled up beside Braddock. He whispered, "You were just trying to spook them, to make them run and give us a chance to get away!"

"You said it yourself," Braddock replied. "Nobody could make a shot like that." He drew a bead again on the cylinder with the shotgun shell stuck in the end. "They don't know how many bullets we've got. Let's see if we can hurry the rest of 'em on their way..."

His finger tightened slowly and smoothly on the trigger. The Colt boomed.

The world blew up.

13

THAT WAS WHAT IT SEEMED LIKE TO BRADDOCK, ANYWAY. A ball of fire erupted and swallowed all three wagons. The ground heaved violently where he lay. The sound was like the loudest crash of thunder he had ever heard. He closed his eyes, ducked his head, and covered it with his arms as gravel and debris pelted him like a hailstorm.

His ears were still ringing when he lifted his head and opened his eyes to take a look at the destruction. A few burning pieces of the wagons were scattered around but, for the most part, the vehicles had vanished. A smoking crater ten feet across marked the spot where the dynamite had been.

Braddock didn't see any bodies. The remaining gunmen who'd been caught in that blast...well, there wouldn't be enough left of them to bury, he thought.

Manuel Santiago pounded Braddock's shoulder in a frenzy. The young man cried, "You did it! You really did it!"

It was mostly blind luck that had guided his second shot to the shell wedged into the stick of dynamite,

Braddock knew, but luck could kill a man—or save him —just as much as anything else.

Right now, he'd take it.

He climbed to his feet and took the shotgun from Manuel. The weapon still had one loaded barrel and Braddock had Paco's Bowie knife, too. He said, "I'm going to take a look and make sure none of the other guards are still around. You get those men out into the open where they'll be safe. It's still possible some of that dynamite in the mine might blow."

Manuel nodded his understanding and hurried back to the other men. Braddock stalked out of the tunnel and held the shotgun ready in case he needed it.

He didn't. All the gunmen who'd been working for Elena and Horner were either dead or long gone. The ones who had fled probably rode even harder when they heard that explosion, Braddock thought.

But the buggy was gone, too. Braddock had been worried about that. It meant Elena and Santiago were already on their way back across the border with murder on their minds.

All the freed prisoners were milling around outside the mine now. Braddock didn't see Manuel Santiago among them. He wondered where the young man had gone, but then he saw Manuel striding out of the tunnel.

"I risked going back in there to take a look," Manuel reported, coughing and wheezing a little. "Paco and the other guards are all dead. The smoke was very thick. I think it must have killed them." He paused, then added, "I'm sorry about Paco. He was a good man once, before my sister bent him to her will. The others..." Manuel spat. "Just gringo outlaws."

"Your sister's not here anymore," Braddock said. "She

and Horner were going to Rainey's ranch to kill him and his son. I've got to try to stop them."

He had already spotted his dun in the corral and knew the rangy horse could cut into the lead Elena and Horner had. Whether he could catch up to them before they reached Rainey's headquarters was the big question.

"I'm coming with you," Manuel said.

"I'm not sure that's a good idea—"

"You think I will betray you when we get there because Elena is my sister?" Manuel shook his head. "She is not the little niña I grew up with. Not anymore. Our father's death, the things that have happened since then...They turned her into someone else. She must be stopped before she commits any more murders."

"You're talking about the way she planned that ambush with Horner?"

"She was *there* that night," Manuel said. "She boasted of it to me, taunted me for being weak while she was strong enough to pull a trigger and kill to avenge our father."

The corner of Braddock's mouth quirked in a grimace. He said, "I'm sorry. Grief and hate can do some mighty bad things to a person. But if we're going to stop them, we've got to get moving."

"I'll go to the bunk house where the guards slept and see if I can find some guns and cartridges."

"I'll saddle my horse and another one," Braddock said.

A few minutes later, when Braddock had the horses saddled and ready to ride, Manuel came back carrying two Winchesters. He had a Colt stuffed in his waistband. A pair of bandoliers filled with cartridges were draped over his shoulder.

He handed a rifle and one of the bandoliers to Braddock. Within moments, all the guns were fully loaded.

Braddock inclined his head toward the group of miners and asked, "What about them?"

"I told them to go into the hills and hide," Manuel said. "They'll watch to see who comes back. If it's one of us, they'll know they're safe." His voice took on a bleak edge as he went on, "If it's my sister or Horner, they know to scatter and return to their homes the best they can."

"All right," Braddock said. He slid the rifle into the saddle boot and swung up onto the dun's back. "Let's go see if we can put a stop to this before it gets any worse."

THEY RODE HARD but they had to slow now and then to keep the horses from getting played out. When they did, they talked.

"My sister has good reason to hate Jason Rainey," Manuel said. "We all knew each other for many years. I thought we were friends. But when our father died and Elena went to work in the cantina, Jason came and, well, paid her to be with him. It was an even greater shame than when she went with others. He had no right to take advantage of her that way, just because he could."

"Did you know she was working there?" Braddock asked.

"Not at first. I got a job as a vaquero on one of the other ranches in the area, so I wasn't around all the time. When I found out, I was furious. I told Elena she could not work there, that what she was doing was a disgrace to our family." Manuel shook his head. "She laughed in my face and told me she would do whatever she had to in order to get what she wanted. I didn't know then that she meant revenge on Martin Rainey but that was the first time I realized my sister had changed and might never be the same again."

Elena wouldn't be the same again, Braddock thought. There was no way a person could do the things she had done and come back from them to be normal again.

Elena was a cold-blooded killer. Manuel would have to deal with that.

And so would Braddock.

After a minute or so, Braddock said, "I've been wondering if Rainey had anything to do with the rustling that ruined your father. There's a man on his crew named Happy Jack Conover who's well known to be a widelooper and brand-blotter. Ramrodding something like that would be right in his wheelhouse."

"I don't know, Señor Braddock. I tried to trail the thieves a few times. I heard many rumors that the stolen cattle were being taken across the Rio Grande to be sold but there was no proof of anything."

"I'm going to try to get to the bottom of that," Braddock promised. "If I get the chance."

If Elena and Horner haven't already killed Martin Rainey, he thought.

They pushed their horses into a run again, following the canyon toward the border river. When they reached the Rio, they splashed across and kept going. A hot wind hooted and howled in the canyon and, even though Braddock knew that's all it was, he couldn't help but think about all the men who had died here. If he had been the sort to believe in restless spirits crying out for vengeance, that was how they would have sounded.

It was so late now that only a few lights still burned in Cemetery Butte. Even the Palomino was probably shut down for the night by this hour. Braddock and

Manuel skirted the settlement and headed for the trail leading to the top of the butte itself.

They hadn't overtaken Horner and Elena but they had to have shaved quite a bit off the pair's lead. Braddock's hope was that Elena wouldn't be in any hurry to kill Rainey and Jason. She'd want to torment them some first. And Horner would follow her head, Braddock was pretty sure of that.

Even if he and Manuel got there in time, the odds might be against them. Conover was probably still at the ranch and there was no telling how many others from Rainey's crew had been paid off to double-cross him.

A big fight would keep Manuel occupied, though, Braddock mused, and that might be a good thing.

It would leave him free to deal with Elena and Horner without any interference.

The moon had set but the sky was still covered with brilliant stars as Braddock and Manuel started up the trail. The faint gray of false dawn lay in the east. There was enough light for them to see where they were going but they had to slow down some to let the horses pick their way along.

Braddock figured they were about halfway to the top when guns began to boom somewhere above them.

14

HEEDLESS OF THE RISK NOW, BRADDOCK SENT THE DUN charging up the slope. Manuel was close behind him on the other horse. When they reached the top, they saw the ranch house in the distance, ablaze with lights. Muzzle flashes winked around it as well as from the windows.

Gunfire surged up to a crescendo as the fighting intensified. Then it abruptly fell silent and Braddock hauled back on the dun's reins as he thrust out his other arm to stop Manuel.

"Sounds like it's over," he said.

"No!"

Braddock understood why the young man was upset. Either his sister was dead—and she still *was* his sister, no matter what else had happened—or she had added to her tally as a killer. There was no good outcome to be had.

"We have to go over there," Manuel said.

"We are," Braddock told him. "We're just not going to announce we're coming and then charge in there blindly." He started the dun forward at a slower pace. "Come on."

When they were within a few hundred yards of the house, they dismounted, let the reins dangle, and catfooted ahead in the darkness, taking the rifles with them. Braddock saw figures moving around against the lights in the house. Somebody was still alive. It was a matter of finding out who.

As they closed in, they used the outbuildings for cover and stuck to the shadows as much as possible. They were beside the barn when they heard men walking toward them. Braddock and Manuel both froze.

"—head for El Paso with my share," one of the men said. "All that shootin's bound to draw people up here and I'd just as soon be long gone when they find the bodies."

"You don't reckon the law's gonna be after you anyway, when Rainey and the kid turn up dead along with those other rannies and you're nowhere to be found?"

"I'll take my chances," the first man said. "For what Happy Jack paid us, it's worth runnin' a few risks."

"Too bad about the Santiago girl, though."

Beside Braddock, Manuel tensed. Braddock touched his shoulder to warn him to stay still for now.

"Yeah, who'd have thought a gal who looks like that would turn out to be as mean as an Apache?"

"She'll have Rainey and Jason screamin' for death 'fore she's through with them, I'll bet a hat on that."

The two men went on into the barn, probably to get their horses.

So Rainey and Jason were still alive, Braddock thought, but maybe for not much longer if Elena had her way. Or rather, according to what the two hired guns had said, they would live long enough to suffer the agonies of the damned.

The easiest thing would be to let the hardcases ride away. Two fewer to deal with that way. But they were outlaws, killers, and the lawman that Braddock would always be rebelled at that idea. He leaned closer to Manuel and whispered, "We've got to take them without any shooting, so we don't warn the ones still in the house. We'll wait until they ride out, then grab them from behind. They won't be expecting anybody to jump them. All of Rainey's loyal hands were probably killed in all that shooting."

Manuel didn't say anything but Braddock faintly saw his curt nod.

Silently, they moved around the corner of the barn and pressed themselves to its front wall. Braddock watched the house in case any more gunmen came out. He wished he knew how many were in there.

The two in the barn were still talking as they got their horses. Braddock could tell by the sounds when they mounted up and started out. He was ready when they emerged from the barn, riding easy and confident in their saddles.

He lunged and leaped, caught hold of one man, and dragged him out of the saddle. The man let out part of a startled yell that Braddock silenced with a blow from the Colt in his hand.

Close by, Manuel had tackled the other man and knocked him off his horse. They struggled together, a tangled heap of shadows. Then a heavy thud sounded and a man grunted in pain. The dark knot separated into two figures, one prone on the ground, the other climbing to his feet.

Braddock trained the revolver on the man until he was sure it was Manuel Santiago.

"We'll drag them into the barn and tie them up," he

ordered quietly.

When they had done that and led the horses into the barn as well, Braddock considered their next move. They couldn't invade the house without knowing how many men they would face.

It would be better to have this fight in the open, anyway, Braddock decided. He said to Manuel, "You stay here."

"I must see this through to the end," he protested.

"You didn't let me finish. You stay here and let me get over there by the house. When I'm in position, you fire off some shots. That ought to draw out Conover and whoever else is still in there. When they charge out to see what the commotion is, we'll catch 'em in a crossfire."

Manuel nodded slowly, then said, "My sister and Horner will send those other men outside. They will stay with Rainey and Jason."

"Then we'll deal with them last," Braddock said.

He wished there wasn't quite so much light spilling from the windows as he hurried toward the house. One of the outlaws might look out and see him coming. But he reached the corner of the porch without hearing any shouts of alarm through the open front door. Crouched there, he waved at Manuel, who was watching from just inside the barn.

Manuel pointed the Winchester at the stars and cranked off four shots as fast as he could work the rifle's lever, paused, and fired three more times.

Braddock heard angry yelling inside the house. Boots thudded on floorboards. Manuel had pulled back into the shadows where he couldn't be seen and Braddock knew the young man would be reloading, thumbing fresh cartridges into the Winchester to replace the ones he'd fired.

Four men burst out of the house and started toward the barn. Their fists were full of guns.

Braddock straightened, lifted the rifle to his shoulder, and called, "Elevate!"

The killers stopped short and started to wheel around. Braddock opened fire and muzzle flame spouted from the barn at the same time. Slugs ripped into the outlaws.

They weren't going down without a fight, though. Even as they staggered under the bullets' impact, they brought their guns up and triggered wildly. Braddock heard the whipcrack of a slug as it went past his ear. He levered the Winchester again and again. A couple of the outlaws collapsed into bloody heaps. Another doubled over as bullets punched into his guts.

Happy Jack Conover was still on his feet despite the bloodstains blooming on the front of his shirt. He yelled, "You damned Ranger!" as he charged at Braddock with both guns roaring and flaming.

Braddock ignored the bullets whipping around him and slammed lead into the center of Conover's forehead. The outlaw's head jerked back. His guns sagged. But his feet kept moving, so he ran two more steps before momentum pitched him forward on his face. In the light from the house, Braddock saw the huge hole in the back of Conover's head where the bullet had blown its way out.

Silence shrouded the ranch house as the echoes died away.

Braddock knelt at the corner of the porch and reloaded. He listened intently. After two minutes that seemed longer, Charles Horner called from inside the house, "Conover? Jack? Are you out there?"

"Blow out the lamps, you damned fool!"

That order came from Elena.

Moments later, the light began disappearing. Darkness closed in.

Floorboards creaked as someone moved out onto the porch. In the shadows, Braddock could make only a dim shape, a deeper patch of darkness. It didn't really look like a man, though.

That was because it was two men, he realized a second later when Horner called, "Who's out there? You'd better not shoot because I've got Rainey in front of me with a gun at his head!"

From the end of the porch, Braddock said, "If you're as smart as you think you are, Horner, you'll drop that gun and give yourself up."

"Braddock!" Horner sounded genuinely shocked. "But that...that's not possible—"

"It's all over," Braddock cut in. "Sooner you realize that, the better off you'll be."

The shape on the porch twisted toward him. From behind Martin Rainey, Horner said, "Give up and hang? I'm not going to do that."

"As far as I know, you haven't actually killed anybody," Braddock pointed out. "You may have helped plan it but you didn't pull any triggers. And I'm pretty sure Scanlon was dead before you shoved that rock down on him." He paused as he saw another shadow creeping closer to the porch. "You might not hang. It's worth risking a trial."

"And give up my revenge?" Horner's voice was shaky now. "No! No, I won't do it. Martin Rainey has to die for what he did—"

Manuel Santiago leaped onto the porch and crashed into both men. Horner yelled as the collision made him lose his grip on Rainey. Manuel grabbed Rainey and dragged him down to the floor. Braddock straightened, pointed the rifle at the staggering Easterner, and shouted, "Drop it, Horner!"

Horner screamed in pure rage, flung up the pistol in his hand, and jerked the trigger. Flame lanced from the barrel. The shot went wide of Braddock who didn't give him a second chance. The Winchester cracked and Horner flew backward. He lost his balance and fell on his side as the pistol skittered away and fell off the porch.

The buggy burst out from behind the house, hoof-beats pounding from the pair of big horses pulling it. Elena slashed at their rumps with the reins. Braddock swung the rifle in that direction but held his fire as Manuel dashed after the vehicle.

"Elena!" the young man cried. "Elena!"

She ignored him and kept whipping the horses for all she was worth.

Manuel ran toward the barn. Braddock knew he was going to grab one of the saddled horses and go after his sister.

He might have done the same thing, but at that moment Charles Horner groaned and started trying to push himself up from the porch where he had fallen. A few feet away, a dazed Martin Rainey had climbed to his hands and knees.

"You...son of a bitch..." Horner rasped as he started hitching himself toward Rainey. "I'll kill you...with my bare hands..."

"Get away from me, you lunatic!" Rainey said as he fell over on his backside and cringed against the wall. "God, Charles, I always tried to help you—"

"You killed...my father..."

"The Apaches killed your father, just like they killed all those other men!"

"Because you led them...into an ambush!" Horner braced himself with his left hand against the floor and stretched out his right arm. His claw-like right hand reached for Rainey's throat. "You deserve...to die!"

Braddock went up the steps onto the porch. He was about to grab hold of Horner and drag him away from Rainey when Horner's strength finally gave out. The hatred that had kept him alive this long couldn't overcome the blood he had lost. He collapsed and lay there at Rainey's feet, gasping harshly for a second before his final breath rattled in his throat.

"Thank God!" Rainey said as his head sagged back against the wall. "The man was insane!"

Braddock leveled the rifle at Rainey and looked at him over the barrel. Rainey's eyes got big. When Braddock saw that, he realized that the eastern sky really was gray now. Sunrise wasn't far off.

"What...what are you doing, Ranger?" Rainey babbled.

"I've got a question for you," Braddock said. His voice was cold and hard. "Satisfy my curiosity."

Rainey tried bluster. He said, "I don't have to tell you anything! You're a lawman! You can't threaten me like this."

A thin smile stretched across Braddock's lips. He said, "You didn't look at my badge close enough yesterday, Rainey."

"What the devil are you talking about?"

"We're the only ones left alive out here. I can put a bullet in your head and nobody will know Horner or one of his men didn't do it. So tell me...were you responsible for the rustling that ruined Felipe Santiago?"

"No!" Rainey cried raggedly. "I swear I didn't have

anything to do with that. I...I took advantage of it, yes. Some might say I...cheated him. But I didn't send men after his stock. You have to believe me!"

Oddly enough, Braddock did. He thought Rainey was too scared right now to lie. Rainey was a greedy, opportunistic bastard...but there was no law against that.

Braddock lowered the rifle.

Rainey closed his eyes and heaved a sigh of relief. Then his eyes snapped open again and he exclaimed, "Jason!"

"Where is he?"

"I...I don't know. That crazy girl had him—"

Elena was gone, fled in the buggy. But she had been alone as far as Braddock could tell which meant Jason Rainey was probably still in the house.

Braddock stepped inside and called, "Jason?"

A low groan from the parlor answered him. It was still dark inside, despite the growing light outside, so Braddock found a match in his pocket and lit a lamp.

The yellow glow washed over a pool of blood. Braddock grimaced as he looked down at Jason Rainey spread-eagled on the floor.

Jason might live but he wouldn't have any more use for whores at a cantina or saloon. Elena had seen to that.

Even though he barely knew her, Braddock had a hunch she had done it with a dull knife, too.

HE SHOULD HAVE GONE after Elena and Manuel, right away, instead of lingering at the ranch. Braddock knew that. He couldn't trust Manuel to capture Elena. Even if he caught up with her, he might let her go. Despite their clash over her lust for revenge, they were still brother and sister.

Braddock figured Elena would head for Mexico. She didn't know for sure what had happened at the mine, only that Braddock and Manuel had gotten away. She might think she could get help there, that Paco and the other men were still alive. Or she might just want to grab whatever gold she could carry and light a shuck out of there, content with what she had done to Jason even though he and his father were still alive when she took off from the ranch.

All Braddock knew for sure was that his gut was leading toward the Rio Grande—and when he found them in the canyon, he knew his instincts had been right.

It was easy enough to see what had happened. The buggy was on its side. The horses were still hitched to it, lying on the ground kicking feebly in their traces. In their wild flight toward the border, with Elena screaming and slashing at them, one of the horses had tripped and gone down, taking the other one with it and causing the buggy to pile up.

The horse Manuel had taken was there, too, standing with its reins dangling.

Manuel sat cross-legged on the ground not far away, holding Elena against him in his lap and crying as her head lolled loosely and unnaturally on her broken neck. He didn't even look up as Braddock rode past them and kept going south, back to Mexico, back to Esperanza, carrying with him the knowledge that Francisco Guzman's death had been avenged. So, in a way, had Felipe Santiago's.

Cold comfort all around. Justice usually was.

Dawn broke over Buzzard's Canyon.

THE LAST WAR CHIEF

1

HE REMEMBERS THE SCREAMS OF WOMEN, CHILDREN, AND *horses. Especially the horses squealing in agony as they are shot down by the blue-clad soldiers who come thundering down the canyon on their own mounts, the rifles in their hands belching fire and smoke.*

The Comanche are horsemen. The death of the horses means the death of the people.

That death takes longer to find those proud riders who are now a-foot. It steals over them slowly as they are rounded up and herded north and east, like animals themselves, into what was known then as Indian Territory but is now called Okla-homa. Despair saps the life from them, making them a shadow of what they once were, until they might as well not be Comanche.

He was a young man then, when the cavalry brought death to the canyon of the hard wood where his people made their home. A young man, but already a leader of his people, a war chief who had ridden with Quanah at the place the white men called Adobe Walls. What times those had been, before the medicine turned bad—

"Hey. Wake up, you ol' sumbitch. You can't sleep there. Move your red ass."

He tried to lift his head from the plank sidewalk but his strength failed him. He murmured something in his native tongue. More than half asleep, he wasn't sure himself what he was saying.

A booted foot thudded into his ribs and rocked him over onto his side. Pain flooded through him but it was a dull, distant ache as if his senses were too old and feeble for him to really feel it. He managed to lift a gnarled hand and tried to wave away his tormentor.

"Damn it, I done told you before about gettin' drunk and sleepin' on the sidewalk, Pete. You're gonna make me drag you down to the jailhouse and lock you up, ain't you?"

"Pahitti Puuku," the old man said. Greasy gray hair straggled in front of his watery eyes as he finally succeeded in lifting his head. He peered through that screen at the lanky figure of Deputy Hal Vickery.

The deputy leaned closer and asked, "What'd you say?"

"Pahitti Puuku."

"You know I don't understand that redskin lingo."

"It means...Three Horses. It is...my name."

"Yeah, well, I'm gonna keep on callin' you Old Pete like ever'body else in Dinsmore. Now, can you get on your feet and stumble outta here? Because if I have to pick you up, you're goin' to a cell, I can promise you that."

Three Horses was a little more awake and alert now. His head pounded from the whiskey and his side ached from the deputy's kick. But he was a war chief. He had suffered much worse in battle. He put his hands on the planks and pushed.

Deputy Vickery watched impatiently as Three Horses struggled to stand up. After what seemed like a long time, and probably was, the old man was on his feet. He was considerably shorter than the lawman. The width of his shoulders testified to the fact that once he had been a powerful man but the years had stolen much of his strength and caused his flesh to waste away.

At first glance, it seemed that not a single inch of his face was free of wrinkles. He wore denim trousers and a faded blue cotton shirt and, the worst indignity of all, white man's shoes on his feet. Even after all this time, he longed for the supple hide of a good pair of moccasins.

"I am...up," he said.

"Good. Stay that way until you can stumble back to that shack o' yours. Can't have you clutterin' up the boardwalk that way. Hell, it's the Twentieth Century now although I reckon a dumb redskin like you wouldn't know anything about that. Dinsmore's a modern town now."

It was true. The settlement, originally nothing more than a wide place in the trail, now boasted a two-story stone jail and an even bigger courthouse, along with a couple of blocks of businesses along the north side of the street, one of them the drugstore in front of which Three Horses had laid down and gone to sleep. Up at the end of the block was an impressive red-brick building that housed the bank that had been organized a couple of years earlier. Perched at the edge of the South Plains, with the rugged escarpment of the caprock dropping away just east of town, Dinsmore was poised to grow into the biggest town between Fort Worth and Lubbock.

It wasn't the sort of place where a pathetic old drunken Indian was welcome anymore...not that the man everybody called Old Pete had been that welcome to start with. Nobody had ever summoned up the energy to run him off permanently, though.

Three Horses took a stumbling step. Deputy Vickery reached out and took hold of his shoulders to turn him around.

"Your shack's that way," the deputy said. "Now skedaddle. I got things to do."

With the work shoes shuffling along the planks, Three Horses started along the sidewalk.

He saw the men riding in from the direction of the caprock but didn't really pay attention to them until they brought their horses to a stop in the street close to where Three Horses was making his laborious way.

"Look at that, Clete," one of the men said. "That's an old Indian, ain't it?"

"Really old," replied the rider whose name, evidently, was Clete. "Must be a hundred years old."

That showed how much the foolish white man knew. This was Three Horses' fifty-fourth summer. Or his fifty-third. He wasn't sure anymore. White man counted time in odd ways.

"I'm gonna talk to him," the first man said, grinning.

"Jawing with some old redskin isn't why we're here, Riggs."

"Won't take but a minute." Riggs swung a leg over his saddle and dropped lithely to the ground. He stepped up onto the sidewalk and went on, "Hey, chief, how you doin'?"

Three Horses frowned in surprise. How did this white man know he was a chief? There was a time when anyone could have told, from the beadwork on his buckskins and the feathers in his headdress, that he was a leader of his people but the clothes he wore now were very different.

Still, this man recognized him for what he was, and that made Three Horses stand up a little straighter. He blinked several times, then said in the white man's tongue, "It is a good day. I am Pahitti Puuku, last war chief of the Comanche."

The man laughed, then said to his companions, "You hear that? He ain't just a dirty old redskin. We got ourselves an actual war chief here!"

"Come on, Riggs," Clete said. "Get back on your horse."

"I will, I will. I ain't never seen a real Comanche war chief, though." Riggs leaned closer and grinned at Three Horses. "Do a war dance."

"I am not at war," Three Horses said. "And it is the young warriors who dance."

"Well, you ain't young, that's for sure, but I reckon we can do something about the other part." Without warning, Riggs slapped Three Horses across the face. "How about now? Feel like lettin' out a war whoop and doin' a dance?"

Three Horses tried to step around the white man. He muttered, "Leave me alone."

Riggs put a hand on his chest and gave him a shove that made him stagger back a couple of steps. Then the white man slapped Three Horses again.

"You're gonna do a war dance, old man, whether you like it or not."

The second slap had been hard enough to make Three Horses' head swim dizzily. He had to catch hold of one of the posts holding up the wooden awning over the boardwalk to keep himself from falling. Anger tried to well up inside him but he couldn't bring it to the surface. That would have taken too much effort and he was too tired.

"Damn it," Clete said. He swung down from the saddle, handed the reins to one of the other men, and stepped up onto the planks. Three Horses thought Clete might make Riggs leave him alone but, instead, the man swung a fist hard into his stomach. The blow made Three Horses double over and that was too much for him to overcome. He toppled forward onto the planks and lay curled up around the pain in his middle.

"Aw, hell!" Riggs said. "What'd you go and do that for?"

"I figured it was the fastest way to get your mind off this ancient savage," Clete said. "Now come on unless you'd rather ride by yourself from now on."

"Shoot, I never said that. I'm comin'."

Riggs paused just long enough to kick Three Horses, on the other side from where Deputy Vickery had kicked him before. At least the pain was balanced now.

Three Horses didn't know how long he lay there, unable to get up, before the shooting started.

2

Part of Hal Vickery's job as deputy sheriff of Dinsmore County was to keep track of the comings and goings of strangers in the settlement. The town wasn't big enough yet to have its own marshal although some of the businessmen had started talking about it, especially Cyrus McLemore, the president of the bank. The county sheriff was responsible for keeping the peace in town and Sheriff Thane Warner had given that job to Vickery. Warner had two other deputies who helped him take care of trouble elsewhere in the county.

So Vickery was just doing his duty when he took note of the strangers who rode into Dinsmore from the east. He did a quick headcount: eight of them. You usually didn't see that many men riding together on horseback unless they all worked for the same ranch and had come into town to blow off steam on payday.

Today wasn't payday. That was still three days off. It wasn't even a Saturday which sometimes brought more folks into town than usual. It was Tuesday morning, still fairly early.

Vickery frowned as he wondered if he ought to go meet the men and inquire as to the business that had brought them to town. But then one of them said something and the whole bunch stopped. From where he stood leaning against an awning post in the middle of the next block, the deputy couldn't make out the words.

Vickery continued watching as the man who had spoken dismounted and stepped up onto the sidewalk to talk to Old Pete. The Indian's shack was on the eastern edge of town—just out of town, really, almost on the edge of the Caprock—and he'd finally been headed in the right direction. Vickery felt a little bad about losing his temper and kicking Pete. It was just that he had told the old-timer over and over again about getting drunk and falling asleep in public. Folks didn't like that.

Most people in Dinsmore barely tolerated Pete, anyway. He was willing to do any sort of odd job, no matter how unpleasant, and he didn't charge much, so he came in handy if you needed a privy mucked out or some animal carcass removed. Because of that, people put up with his boasting.

When he was drunk, he liked to go on about how he was the last war chief of the Comanche tribe and how he'd fought with ol' Quanah and then snuck off from the reservation up in what used to be Indian Territory. He claimed that all the land hereabouts was the rightful hunting ground of his people and said that they would take it back, one of these days when the buffalo herds returned.

Vickery wasn't going to hold his breath waiting for that to happen.

The stranger who had gotten off his horse was talking to Old Pete. Suddenly, the man slapped him. That was a mean thing to do and it made Vickery's frown deepen as he straightened from his casual stance leaning on the post. Pete might be a smelly, troublesome old fool, but he was *Dinsmore's* smelly, troublesome old fool. No stranger could ride into town and start pushing him around.

Then Vickery hesitated. He had hauled off and kicked Pete not that long ago, after all. He knew how annoying the old Indian could be. Maybe, if the fella would leave him alone, it would be better to just let things go.

Then the man slapped Pete again.

Vickery wasn't going to stand for that. He started along the boardwalk. But he didn't get in too big a hurry about it. Even though it was only mid-morning, the day was already hot and a fella didn't want to rush around too much in the West Texas heat. It wasn't good for the blood.

One of the other men dismounted. Vickery hoped he would take his companion in hand. The whole bunch might move on.

Then the second man punched Pete in the belly, an even more despicable blow than the others. Pete fell down and the first man kicked him. Vickery really felt bad now about what he'd done as he watched somebody else do the same thing. That was pretty sorry behavior.

"Hey!" he called as he stepped off the end of the boardwalk in this block and started across the open space between the buildings. All eight of the strangers turned toward him and he heard the man who had kicked Pete say, "Oh, hell, Riggs, now look what you've done. A lawman."

Vickery was about to say that damn right he was a lawman and he wasn't going to stand for any of Dinsmore's citizens being treated that way but then the second man lifted his arm and there was a gun in his hand, a gun the deputy hadn't even seen him draw. Vickery stopped short as his eyes widened and he reached for the revolver on his hip.

He had just closed his hand around the gun butt when he heard the blast of a shot at the same time as what felt like a sledgehammer struck him in the chest. He went over backward and the act of falling helped him pull his gun from its holster. His arm sort of flew upward of its own accord but he was conscious of pulling the trigger. He heard shots booming like thunderclaps in a spring storm.

That was the last thing he knew.

3

THE SHOTS WERE SO LOUD THEY SEEMED TO SHAKE THE
planks Three Horses was lying on and somehow that
jolted the pain out of him. The racket also blew away the
last lingering effects of the whiskey he had stolen early
that morning while he was sweeping out the Three
Deuces, Dinsmore's only saloon. The place didn't have a
regular swamper but Three Horses swept and mopped
there two or three times a week and Miles Bowen, the
owner, usually turned a blind eye when he snagged a
bottle that still had a little booze in it and tucked it inside
his shirt.

For one thing, when he let Three Horses get away
with that, Bowen usually didn't bother paying him. The
rotgut didn't cost much since Bowen brewed it himself
in an old bathtub, throwing in some black powder,
strychnine, and rattlesnake heads for flavor.

Sober now, or as close to it as he got these days,
Three Horses lifted his head, pushed himself up on his
elbows, and looked along Dinsmore's single street. He
saw somebody lying in the open space between the two

blocks of businesses and he needed a second or two before he recognized the sprawled figure in the bloody shirt as Deputy Hal Vickery.

Despite everything that had happened earlier, Three Horses felt a pang of regret at the sight. Vickery sometimes got mad and treated him badly but the deputy has helped him at times, too, taking pity on him and getting him back to his shack when he was too drunk to make it there under his own power.

The eight strangers—Clete, Riggs, and the other six men—were doing most of the shooting. Four of them, including Clete and Riggs, were standing in front of the bank pouring lead through the windows and the open front door.

The other four were still on their horses as they fired toward the jail. Their mounts were a little skittish, so they had to divide their efforts between controlling the animals and shooting at the stone building.

Little puffs of gunsmoke came from one of the jail's front windows. Three Horses didn't know where the sheriff and the other two deputies were but it seemed likely at least one man was inside, putting up a fight.

Everyone else who had been on the street when the trouble started—and there hadn't been that many—had vanished, immediately hunting cover as the bullets began to fly.

Bill Denning, who owned the drugstore, proved to be the exception to that. He emerged from the front door of his business and stomped along the sidewalk past Three Horses carrying an old Henry rifle. He yelled, "Damn thieves!" and brought the repeater to his shoulder. It cracked once but none of the strangers fell.

One of them on horseback yanked his mount around toward the walk, however, and the revolver in his hand let out two heavy booms. Denning flew backward to land next to Three Horses, who was lying on his belly. The front of the storekeeper's apron Denning wore over his clothes was bloody and a good chunk of his head was blown away. His eyes were wide open as he stared sightlessly up at the awning.

If anybody else in town was thinking about fighting back against the outlaws, the sight of Denning being killed in such a grisly fashion put a stop to that.

Except for Three Horses, who looked over at the Henry the drugstore owner had dropped and felt an unexpected longing.

Years ago, Three Horses had had a rifle like that. He had taken it from a dead settler on a ranch he and some other warriors had raided up on the Double Mountain fork of the Brazos. The weapon had seemed like magic at the time, a gun that could shoot all day without having to be reloaded.

Of course, there was no magic to it—the white men had no real magic—and the Comanches had figured that out and soon lost their fear of the repeaters. In fact, many warriors had become quite proficient in their use.

Three Horses had been good with a rifle. But he recalled how heavy a Henry was and how his hands shook and the muscles in his arms trembled when he tried to lift too much these days, and he decided it wouldn't be a good idea.

Just to be sure none of the outlaws would think he had anything in mind, he let his head droop back to the planks and lay there like he was senseless.

He kept his eyes slitted open, though, and watched as Clete and Riggs and the other two men on foot rushed into the bank. They must have killed everyone inside, thought Three Horses.

Then two more shots sounded, first one and then a second blast a couple of heartbeats later, and Three Horses thought, no, *now* they have killed everyone.

The shooting from the jail stopped as well. An echoing silence hung over the settlement. A minute went by. Two. Three.

Then Clete and Riggs and the other two ran out of the bank. Clete had a gun in each hand but the others each carried a pair of canvas sacks. Three Horses knew the bags were full of money.

He frowned as he forced his brain to work. Was payday coming up soon? It was, he decided. The bank usually had plenty of cash on hand for that since there were a number of large ranches in the area with big crews that collected wages once a month.

Working quickly, without any wasted effort, the outlaws tied the money bags to their saddles and swung up. Clete, who seemed to be the leader, was the last one in the saddle. He pouched his left-hand iron and grabbed the reins, swinging his horse around and jabbing his boot heels in its flanks.

The entire gang galloped toward Three Horses.

He was convinced they were going to shoot him as they raced past. Terror gnawed at his guts.

Then, he felt something different and realized it was shame burning inside him because he was afraid. There had been a time when he felt no fear even when he was facing many enemies. If he was truly a warrior, truly a man, he told himself, he would take that rifle and stand up and fight...

The outlaws veered into the open space between the blocks, making the turn with the skill of expert horse-men, and charged out of town as if they intended to head north along the Caprock. As they did, the steel-shod hooves of their mounts chopped and pounded the body of Deputy Hal Vickery until it looked like a heap of bloody rags instead of something human.

Then they were gone, the swift rataplan of hoofbeats fading into the distance.

Three Horses heard someone weeping. He had to think about it for a while before he realized the wretched sounds came from him. He didn't know if he was crying for Deputy Vickery and everyone else the strangers had killed in Dinsmore on this hot Tuesday morning or for himself because they had humiliated him and he had done nothing about it except lie there and wallow in his own fear.

It was a bad day for the once-proud Comanche people when their last war chief acted that way, he thought. The latest bad day in a very long line of them.

4

G.W. BRADDOCK WAS A LONG WAY FROM THE BORDER. Too far for safety, really. Despite the badge pinned to his faded blue bib-front shirt, he was a wanted man on this side of the Rio Grande.

An outlaw, not a Texas Ranger anymore.

But that didn't mean he could stop enforcing the law. It was the job he had been raised to do, after all, and no amount of political shenanigans designed to cripple the Ranger force could change that.

These days, he had a home of sorts in the Mexican village of Esperanza, just across the border. The priest at the mission there had nursed Braddock back to health from the wounds he had received defending the village from marauders. The little, brown-robed padre was the closest thing Braddock had to a friend in this world, he supposed.

From time to time, when word reached the village of trouble in Texas, Braddock pinned on the star-in-a-circle badge carved from a Mexican *cinco peso* coin and rode back across the river to the land of his birth, the land he had been raised to serve. The most recent occasion had been several weeks earlier. One of the farmers from the village had ventured downriver to Del Rio to sell some crops on the Texas side and he had returned to Esperanza with the tale of how a gang of vicious outlaws had robbed the bank there while the farmer was in town.

The leader of the gang, it was said, was a man named Clete Fenner.

Braddock knew the name, even though he had never crossed trails with the desperado. He remembered seeing it in the Doomsday Book, the Ranger "bible" that listed all the known lawbreakers in the state.

It was time that name was crossed out of the book, Braddock had decided. When he heard how wantonly Fenner and his men had shot up Del Rio, that made up his mind for him. That group of mad dogs had to be stopped.

Braddock had picked up the trail without much trouble, but closing in on Fenner's gang was a different story. Somehow, the outlaws managed to stay one or two jumps ahead of him, even when they stopped long enough to hit a bank or rob a stagecoach or steal some fresh horses from a ranch.

They left a trail of bodies behind them, as well, and each brutal, senseless death added to Braddock's resolve. He would bring the killers to justice no matter how far he had to follow them.

That was how he wound up several hundred miles north of the border, riding northwest as he approached the Caprock, the line of rugged bluffs that ran in irregular fashion through this region, dividing Central Texas from the windswept plains that stretched all the way from here to New Mexico Territory. Fenner and his men had been spotted heading in this direction, following the wagon road.

Wherever they were bound for, they wouldn't have anything good in mind when they got there.

The trail dropped down into a little depression just this side of the escarpment, then started up. The rocky bluff was dotted with brush but lots of bare ground showed through as well. In the midday sun, the red clay common to this area was vividly bright. Up on the plains, it would be a different story, Braddock knew. The soil there was sandier, more thickly covered with vegetation lying close to the ground. It was good grazing land although it became more arid the farther west a man went.

The climb was steep in places as the trail twisted back and forth but not too steep for a horse. Braddock reached the top and reined in as he saw a settlement lying less than half a mile away. A lot of people were moving around in the single street, he thought as a slight frown creased his forehead. More than seemed normal even though it was the middle of the day and folks might be out and about.

He heeled the dun forward.

Braddock had the broad shoulders and lean hips of a born horseman. A lot of time spent in the saddle as he chased badmen around Texas had allowed the sun to bestow a brown, leathery look to his face. It had faded his hair and mustache to a sandy color. A scar on his forehead disappeared up under his darker brown hat. A saber belonging to a crazed *rurale capitan* had left the mark there.

Like the hat, his clothes were typical dust-covered

range garb. He wore a Colt .45 in a holster on his right hip and the well-worn wooden stock of a Winchester repeater stuck up from a sheath lashed to his saddle.

The only bright thing about him was the Ranger badge. It glittered in the sun. When people saw it, they recognized the authority it carried and tended not to notice the small, neat bullet hole in the center of it, a souvenir from another encounter with a killer. They assumed that Braddock was still an official lawman, not an outlaw, and it suited his purposes not to correct that assumption.

He had to be careful about other star-packers, though. Often, they were more alert and suspicious than civilians.

But not the one Braddock found in this settlement. This one was running around like a chicken with its head cut off.

The man was a little below medium height and stocky. His round face had what looked like a permanent sunburn. That went with the blue eyes and the fair hair under a thumbed-back hat. He had a badge pinned to his shirt.

When he spotted Braddock, he stopped hurrying around among the various groups of townspeople in the street and on the plank sidewalk. A look of relief came over his face. He started walking toward Braddock and was almost running by the time he got there.

"You're a Ranger?" the man said. "A Texas Ranger?"

"That's right," Braddock said. In his heart, he would always be a Ranger, no matter what the official records in Austin said. Now that he was closer, he could read the words *DEPUTY SHERIFF* etched on the tin star. "What happened here, Deputy?"

The man took off his hat and scrubbed a pudgy-fingered hand over his flushed face. He heaved a sigh as if exhaustion were catching up to him.

"Bank robbers," he said. "A gang of outlaws hit the bank about an hour ago."

"Anybody hurt?" asked Braddock.

"They killed seven people, including Sheriff Warner and Deputy Vickery," the man replied. "My name's Andy Bell. I'm the only law left here in Dinsmore. At least, I was until you showed up, Ranger...?"

"Braddock," he introduced himself curtly. "Dinsmore is the name of this settlement?"

"Yeah."

"I've heard of it, I reckon. Never been here before that I recall." Braddock nodded toward the stone courthouse. "It's the county seat, I see."

"Yeah. The biggest town in the county. And the only one with a bank." Deputy Bell made a face. "I reckon that's why those sons o' bitches came here."

"How many of them were there?"

"Eight or ten. I've gotten different answers from people. It's hard to keep count when something like that's going on. They shot Deputy Vickery first." Bell pointed to a blanket-shrouded figure lying in the street between the two blocks of businesses. A couple of booted feet stuck out from under the blanket. "Then some of them opened fire on the sheriff's office and jail while the others shot through the bank's front windows until everybody inside was either dead or wounded. They went in then and cleaned out the cash drawers and the vault and...and finished off the wounded."

"The vault was open?" Braddock asked.

Deputy Bell shrugged and said, "This is a little town.

Nothing like this ever happened here. Nobody figured it ever would." Bell paused and swallowed hard. "They didn't have to kill everybody. They could have gone in, held up the place at gunpoint, and gotten the money if that was all they were after. It was like they...they *wanted* to slaughter innocent people."

"This gang...was the leader named Fenner? Clete Fenner?"

Bell's shoulders rose and fell in a shrug.

"Mister, I just couldn't tell you. I don't know if anybody heard any of them call the others by name. I've been askin' questions but it all happened so fast and, like I told you, nobody ever expected anything like this..."

Braddock held up a hand to stop Bell before the deputy could force himself to go on. Bell might be fine for serving legal papers or guarding prisoners but, when faced with a real catastrophe, he didn't seem like much of a lawman.

But maybe he shouldn't judge people, Braddock told himself. After all, at least Bell had a legal right to wear his badge.

"You say the sheriff was killed?"

"Yes, sir. When he heard the commotion going on outside, he stepped through the door to find out what it was all about and caught a couple of slugs in the chest right away. He fell in the doorway and I was able to get hold of his shirt and drag him the rest of the way back inside without getting shot myself." Bell shook his head. "Wasn't anything I could do for him, though. He was already gone. All I could do was fort up at one of the windows and try to wing some of that bunch but I don't know if I did or not. They made it pretty hot for me."

"Who else was killed?"

"Like I said, the folks in the bank. Mr. McLemore, the president, and Ben Horton, the teller, along with a couple of customers. And Mr. Denning, who owned the drugstore. He came out and took a shot at 'em, and they gunned him down, just shot him like a dog."

Braddock said, "I'll bet nobody put up a fight after that, did they?"

"No, sir, they did not. And I, for one, don't really blame 'em."

"Didn't say I blamed them. They just would have gotten themselves killed if they had without doing anybody else any good. From the sound of it, that was the Fenner gang, all right. I've been on their trail for weeks. I could count up the number of people they've killed, I suppose, but it would make me a little sick."

"So you're going after them?" Deputy Bell asked. Braddock heard an almost pathetic eagerness in the man's voice. If a Texas Ranger took over the pursuit, that would relieve Bell of the responsibility for doing so.

"Like I said, I've been on their trail. This just makes me more determined than ever to catch up to them. You haven't put together a posse yet, have you?"

"No, I was just thinking about gettin' around to doing that..."

"Don't," Braddock said.

Bell frowned and said, "I beg your pardon?"

"I'll go after them alone. I don't need a posse."

What Braddock meant but didn't say was that he didn't need a posse slowing him down and cluttering things up. He could move faster alone and he wouldn't have to worry about a bunch of inexperienced townies getting themselves killed when he finally caught up to Fenner's bunch.

"Are you sure? I mean, it was our town they hit, our bank they robbed. Our people they killed—"

"They've done the same thing across a wide swath of Texas. Don't worry, they'll get what's coming to them."

"But...but it'll be eight or ten to one..."

"Long odds never bothered me," Braddock said.

An outlaw Ranger couldn't expect to live forever.

5

The long journey had depleted Braddock's supplies so he figured it would be a good idea to replenish them here in Dinsmore before setting off after Clete Fenner and his gang. If his pursuit of the outlaws had taught him anything, it was that he couldn't predict how long it was going to take him to corral them.

Several of Dinsmore's citizens came up to him while he was in the general store and offered to come with him. Word had gotten around quickly that there was a Texas Ranger in town who planned to go after the bank robbers.

Braddock refused the offers of assistance as diplomatically as he could but he knew he was a little curt to some of the men. He couldn't worry about that. Time was a-wasting. With every minute that passed, the bloodthirsty gang would be getting farther away.

So he was in no mood to be delayed when he stepped out onto the sidewalk in front of the store with a canvas sack of supplies in his hand and an old-timer waiting there lifted a trembling hand to stop him.

"Ranger," the man said. "I must talk to you."

With the old man blocking his path, Braddock had no choice but to stop. He saw that the man was an Indian and realized he might not be as quite as old as Braddock had thought at first. Or he might be older. With all those wrinkles in the weathered skin, it was hard to tell. The fellow might have been anywhere from fifty to eighty.

"I'm in a hurry—" Braddock began.

"You are going after the man called Clete?"

That question made Braddock frown for a second. He said, "How do you know one of them was named Clete?"

Of course, he had mentioned the name to Deputy Bell, he recalled, and he didn't know who Bell might have told. The old Indian could have heard it that way.

"I heard one of them say it," the old-timer replied. "And Clete called that one Riggs."

Braddock's interest quickened. This leathery old cuss might know something useful after all.

"You heard them talking to each other?"

"They spoke...to me." The old man rested his right hand against his narrow chest with the fingers splayed out.

"What did they say?"

"The one called Riggs, he asked me to do a war dance."

"Why would he do that?" asked Braddock.

"Because I am Three Horses, last war chief of the Comanche."

Braddock managed not to snort in disbelief. The old man was short and wiry. Scrawny might have been a better description. He wore a ragged work shirt and trousers and scuffed shoes that probably had holes in the soles. Shaggy gray hair hung over his eyes and ears. He looked about as far from being a war chief as anybody could get.

"Did you hear them say anything about where they were headed from here?"

Three Horses, if that was really his name, shook his head.

"No. Riggs slapped me, to try to get me to dance, and then the one called Clete, he hit me, too, and knocked me down so Riggs would leave me alone. Clete was angry and told him they had to get on with their business."

Yeah, the business of robbing the bank and murdering half a dozen innocent people, thought Braddock.

"I saw what they did," Three Horses went on. "After Clete knocked me down, I was lying on the sidewalk, there, in front of the drugstore where Mr. Denning was killed. I did not get up."

Braddock grunted and said, "Good thing you didn't. They probably would've shot you, too."

"I looked at the rifle Mr. Denning had. I thought about fighting them. I could have done it." Three Horses looked down at the sidewalk. "But I did nothing."

"Well, that's all right, old-timer. Fighting outlaws isn't your job. It's mine."

Braddock moved to step around him but, once again, the old Indian lifted a hand to stop him.

"Among my people, I was always one of the best trackers. On the hunt, I could follow prey across many miles." Three Horses made a sweeping gesture with his hand, like a Wild West Show Indian putting on a show. "No enemy ever escaped me once I had found his trail. I will come with you, Ranger, and help you track down these evil men."

The offer took Braddock by surprise. The Indian looked like he was barely strong enough to walk down the street, let alone trail a gang of vicious killers across the plains.

"I appreciate that," Braddock said, "but you don't need to—"

Three Horses moved closer and said, "They struck me. They knocked me down and then they kicked me like I was a mongrel dog that had slunk in their way. They did this to me, Three Horses, last war chief of the Comanche." He drew himself up straighter and glared. "They must be punished."

"Yeah, well, I plan to see to it," Braddock told him. "You can count on that. But I don't need any help."

"There are eight of them," Three Horses said with conviction.

"You're sure of that?"

"I counted them. Four attacked the bank, the other four attacked the sheriff's office."

That jibed well enough with what Deputy Bell had told him, Braddock thought. He was willing to accept what Three Horses said about how many outlaws there had been, although it didn't really change things one way or the other.

However many there were, Braddock still had to bring them to justice or die trying.

"Thanks anyway, Three Horses, but I ride alone."

"Because of that?"

The old man pointed at the badge on Braddock's shirt. Braddock frowned and said, "What do you mean?"

"The hole in that badge...it means you are apart from all the other Rangers. Is this not true?"

Braddock started to brush past him, muttering, "I've got to get riding—"

"You are the only one of your kind," Three Horses persisted, "just as I am the last war chief of my people. That is why you ride alone. Perhaps two who ride alone...should ride together."

"Forget it," Braddock said. He headed for the dun. "Go back to whatever it is you do around here."

Behind him, Three Horses was silent.

Deputy Bell came up while Braddock was tying the supplies behind his saddle. The lawman said, "Are you sure you don't want me to come with you, Ranger?"

"No, you don't need to leave the town without any law. After a tragedy like this, folks need to see that there's still somebody in charge."

"I never thought that'd be me," Bell said. He took a bandanna from his pocket and wiped sweat off his face. "I'm the youngest of the three deputies. Hal Vickery, he was in charge of keepin' order here in town, and he's dead. Gene Dixon, he's chief deputy. Sheriff Warner sent him down to the southern part of the county to look for some cattle thieves. Probably won't be back for a few days. That just leaves me."

"You'll be fine," Braddock told him, although in truth he hoped that nothing else bad happened in Dinsmore until that older deputy got back. Bell might find himself over his head pretty easily.

The deputy didn't look convinced by Braddock's reassurances but he said, "I saw Old Pete talking to you. Sorry if he bothered you."

"The old Indian? He said his name was Three Horses."

"Yeah, but most of the time he spouts the Comanche version of it and nobody can pronounce that so folks started calling him Old Pete. Maybe that other name means Three Horses but you couldn't prove it by me. I don't speak Comanch'."

Braddock said, "Was he really a war chief?"

"Who the hell knows? You've seen him. He's just a drunken old sot and a part-time handyman. Showed up here about five years ago and he's been hanging around ever since, making a pest of himself. What did he want, anyway?"

"He wanted to come with me. Wanted to help me track Fenner and his gang."

Bell's pale eyebrows went up as he said, "You're not taking him along, are you?"

"Not hardly," Braddock said.

6

THE CAPROCK ROSE ANYWHERE FROM FIVE HUNDRED TO two thousand feet above the rolling, scrub-covered terrain to the east. The outlaws' trail ran close enough to the rim that Braddock had a spectacular view in that direction. Some people might say the landscape was ugly but Braddock found a stark beauty in it. He was a Texan, born, bred, and forever, and just about everywhere in the Lone Star State had something to recommend it as far as he was concerned.

There wasn't much in the direction he was headed except some isolated ranches. Maybe Fenner and his gang were going to ground at long last, after their bloody trek from the border country. With all the robberies they had carried out, they had to have a pretty good stash of loot by now. They might hole up somewhere, wait for any pursuit to die down, and then venture out to enjoy their ill-gotten gains somewhere like Denver or San Francisco.

They might even scatter to the four winds which

would make it extremely difficult to track down all of them. Braddock wanted to catch up to the gang before that could happen. He pushed the dun as fast as he dared. The horse had covered a lot of ground in the past few weeks, however, and Braddock couldn't risk asking too much of him.

Red sandstone boulders littered the edge of the Caprock in places and fissures cut into the escarpment's face. It was rugged country that could hide a lot of dangers and Braddock was well aware of that and kept his eyes open.

Because he was alert, he saw afternoon sunlight reflect off something metal among a clump of large rock slabs. Letting his instincts take over instead of thinking about it, he leaned forward in the saddle and jabbed his boot heels in the dun's flanks. The horse leaped forward as a rifle cracked. Braddock heard a bullet whine just behind him as it ripped through the space where he had been a split-second earlier.

More shots crashed as Braddock galloped toward the nearest cover, some low rocks less than half as big as the boulders where the would-be killers were concealed. They had chosen a good spot for their ambush. The ground was bare and open except for some small mesquite trees that wouldn't really provide much concealment or stop bullets. The rocks were Braddock's only chance. He couldn't hope to outrun rifles.

Bullets kicked up dust around the dun's flashing hooves. Since they had missed their first couple of shots at him, they were trying to shoot the horse out from under him, Braddock knew. If they were able to do that, then they could pick him off at their leisure.

The dun was moving so fast it made a difficult target,

though. The horse jumped a little as a slug burned across its rump but that was the closest any of the bullets came. As they neared the rocks, Braddock pulled his Winchester from the saddle boot, kicked his feet free of the stirrups, and dived off the horse's back.

He lost his hat as he flew through the air. He landed running, lost his balance, went down, and rolled. A bullet whistled past his ear as he came up and lunged forward to stretch out on his belly among the rocks.

He hoped there weren't any rattlesnakes sunning themselves in there. Even if there were, they might be better company than a bunch of hot lead.

Braddock didn't hear any of the telltale buzzing that would have let him know he had scaly companions in this precarious sanctuary. Of course, the blood was pounding pretty loudly in his head by now, drowning out just about everything else. But as his pulse slowed, he heard the shots from the boulders about fifty yards away, the thud as bullets struck the rocks that protected him, and the occasional whine as a slug ricocheted off.

As long as he kept his head down, he was safe. Enough rocks were scattered around him to keep the bushwhackers from having a clear shot at him.

They must have realized they were wasting lead because their rifles fell silent. Braddock lay there breathing hard as tense seconds crawled past.

They were trying to bait him into making a move, he thought. From the sounds of the shots, two men were hidden in the boulders and he'd be willing to bet that both of them had their rifles aimed at the spot where he had disappeared. Their fingers would be tight on the triggers. If he raised his head, even for a second, they would fire, and it was even money whether or not they would blow his brains out.

So it was a waiting game. Braddock was pinned down, sure but a glance at the sky told him there were only about five hours of daylight left. He would get mighty hot and thirsty in that time, baking here under the sun, but it wouldn't kill him. And when night fell, he would be able to move again.

He twisted his head around to look for his horse. The dun had kept running for about a quarter of a mile before coming to a stop. He stood there now, grazing aimlessly on clumps of hardy grass. At least the bushwhackers weren't shooting at him anymore. No reason to kill a perfectly good horse when his rider was the real target and that rider was no longer in the saddle.

Two men, Braddock mused as the back of his neck began to get warm. Hidden in the boulders along the rim like that, it was obvious they had been waiting for someone to come along. Him in particular? Braddock doubted it. More likely Clete Fenner had left a couple members of the gang to discourage any posse from Dinsmore that had followed them.

Braddock was only one man, not a posse, but maybe they had spotted him through field glasses and seen the badge on his shirt. They would know he was a lawman. They might have even figured out it was a Ranger badge.

Might have been better not to wear the thing, but it was part of who he was. That was why he had refused to turn it in or give up enforcing the law, the job he was born for, no matter what some judge or politician said.

Damn, the sun was hot, even though it wasn't directly overhead. Braddock wondered how much time had gone by. Seemed like an hour but he knew that probably only a few minutes had passed.

If the two bushwhackers really wanted him dead, they would have to make a move before dark. They couldn't afford to just squat there in the boulders and wait. More than likely, one of them would try to flank him, move around so that he had a clear shot. Braddock listened intently for any sound that might warn him that was happening.

Suddenly, shots boomed out again, the echoes rolling across the Caprock and the valleys below. A distraction, thought Braddock. One of the killers was on the move.

He twisted, using his elbows and toes to wiggle himself over to a narrow gap between the rocks. He thrust the Winchester's barrel through the opening and waited. He knew it was fifty-fifty that the outlaw would go that direction and, even if he did, Braddock would have only a split-second to fire.

A flash of movement in the distance. Braddock had already taken the slight bit of slack out of the trigger. He squeezed it the rest of the way. The Winchester cracked wickedly as it bucked against his shoulder.

The shots from the boulders stopped. Braddock heard a man yelling in pain. A faint smile tugged at his lips under the mustache. Instinct—and one hell of a lot of luck, to be honest—must have guided his shot. He edged forward, trying to see if he could spot the man he had wounded, but his field of vision was too small, the angle too restricted.

A few moments later, both rifles opened up on his position again. The man he had winged must not have been hurt too badly. He had retreated into the boulders and joined his companion in an angry fusillade at the rocks where Braddock had taken cover. They were just venting their spleen. They still couldn't get a good shot at him.

Then he heard a boom and a startled shout. Braddock knew from the sound of the earlier reports that the bushwhackers were using Winchesters or Henrys. That shot hadn't come from a repeater. It had sounded more like a heavy-caliber buffalo gun.

Somebody else was getting in on this fight.

The question was, on which side?

7

From the door of his tar-paper shack, Three Horses watched the Ranger ride out of Dinsmore, heading north along the edge of the Caprock on the trail of the outlaws.

The Ranger had made a mistake. He should have accepted Three Horses' help. Three Horses was a tracker and a warrior. He would have given his life to help bring those men to justice.

Maybe he still could.

He turned and went to the bunk where he slept on a bare corn-shuck mattress. Bending over, he reached under the bunk and pulled out a rifle. It was very old. Rust pitted its barrel and, at some time in the past, its stock had been cracked and then mended by having wire wrapped tightly around it. The breech and the bore were clean, though. Three Horses used a rag and a stick every day to wipe away the red dust that got into everything.

Many years earlier, the rifle had belonged to a buffalo hunter, a huge, bearded, shaggy man who resembled the beasts he stalked and slew. During a battle with a group of hunters who had taken cover in a buffalo wallow,

Three Horses had counted coup on the man, then turned his pony to race back in and put an arrow through his throat. He had taken the rifle, which he had thought of then as a shoots-far-gun, as his by right since he had killed its owner, just like the Henry he had taken from a dead rancher several years later.

By now he knew it was a .50 caliber Sharps. He had shot it a few times and never liked it but he had wrapped it in a blanket and hidden it among the few possessions he'd been allowed to take along when his people were herded northeast to the reservation in Indian Territory. He could not have said why he hung on to it, other than the fact that he sensed there was powerful medicine in it and, one day, that medicine would be revealed to him.

All he was certain of was that he could not leave it behind when he fled the reservation. He reached under the bunk again and pulled out the other thing he had brought with him, a white man's carpetbag filled with even more precious possessions.

He felt stronger now. The whiskey had sweated out through his skin. When he held his hands in front of his face, they trembled, but only a little.

Could he do this? Three Horses had to admit he didn't know. But he had to try.

Carrying the Sharps in his left hand and the carpetbag in his right, he walked back into town to the livery stable owned by Asa Edmonds. From time to time, Three Horses cleaned the stalls for Mr. Edmonds. He found the man sitting on a barrel just outside the barn's open double doors.

"Howdy, Pete," Edmonds said. "Hell of a thing, wasn't it? The way those outlaws came in and killed so many folks, I mean."

"Yes," Three Horses agreed. "A hell of a thing."

His people, as a rule, didn't curse but you had to talk to white men in a language they understood.

Edmonds frowned at the carpetbag and the rifle. He asked, "You goin' somewhere? Takin' a trip?"

"Yes, I must leave Dinsmore for a time."

"Goin' back to the reservation?" The liveryman grinned. "You ain't goin' on the warpath, are you?"

"There is something I have to do."

"Well, don't let me stop you. You just go right ahead." Edmonds chuckled as if the idea of an Indian having anything important to do amused him.

"I would like to borrow the mule, the one called Abner."

A frown replaced Edmonds' grin as he said, "Wait a minute. You want to borrow my mule? You mean rent it, don't you? I ain't in the business of lettin' folks *borrow* my animals."

Three Horses shook his head and said, "You know I have no money. But I will give you something in return for the loan of the mule."

He set the carpetbag down, leaned the Sharps against the wall, and opened the bag to take out a tomahawk. Its handle was decorated with bits of brightly colored rock and feathers tied on with rawhide.

Edmonds' eyes opened wider as he said, "That looks real."

"It is real. It belonged to Satanta. He gave it to me himself, for saving his life during a battle with the blue-coats, before they took him later on and hung him."

That was a lie in more ways than one. Three Horses had made the tomahawk himself, just to pass the time during the dreary days on the reservation. He had never met the notorious warrior Satanta.

But Edmonds didn't know that and he let out a low

whistle.

"You're sayin' you'll gimme that if I let you borrow Abner?"

Three Horses nodded and said solemnly, "Yes."

"But I don't have to return it, even when you bring Abner back."

"That is right. It is yours."

Three Horses held out the tomahawk and the liveryman took it.

"You got yourself a deal," Edmonds said.

"You will provide a saddle, too?"

Edmonds frowned and said, "Dang, there must be somethin' to that idea that you Injuns are related to the Jews, the way you like to haggle. Ah, hell, sure, I'll throw in a saddle. Just not one of the good ones. Get one of 'em that's set aside in the tack room. You know the ones I mean."

Three Horses nodded and walked into the welcome shade of the barn. He went to the stall where Edmonds kept the mule Abner and led the animal out. Mules were supposed to be balky but Abner and Three Horses had always gotten along well and Abner cooperated now. Three Horses got a ratty blanket and a saddle that needed mending from the tack room and soon had Abner ready to ride.

Edmonds was still sitting on the barrel, turning the tomahawk over in his hands. He looked up at Three Horses and said, "I've figured it out. You're gonna go hunt buffalo."

"When I hunted buffalo, I used a bow and arrow, not a gun."

"What's the rifle for, then?"

"To hunt men," Three Horses said.

He rode off and left the liveryman staring after him.

8

IT WAS AMAZING HOW MUCH A MAN COULD CHANGE IN
less than a day's time. A matter of hours, really. When he
had climbed out of his bunk this morning, Three Horses
hadn't expected anything other than one more day of
struggling to get by as he battled the demons inside him.
One more day of cadging drinks, one more day of doing
menial labor if he could find anyone willing to hire him,
one more day of being humiliated and laughed at by
people who didn't believe him when he told them what
he had been in the past.

He had been humiliated and laughed at, all right, but
he had also been beaten and kicked like a dog. He had
stared into the face of death only inches from his when
the outlaw killed Denning. He had seen blood spilled
and heard the cries of the grieving. He had felt the worm
of fear inside him, eating away at his soul.

In the past, when anything this upsetting had
happened, Three Horses had sought solace in a bottle.
Solace and forgetfulness. There was nothing like

whiskey to numb the pain of a man's pride as it slowly withered away.

So why was today different, he wondered as he rode along the rim of the Caprock? Perhaps some men reached the end of their rope and died, as he had expected to, while others grasped that rope and used it to pull themselves up.

Which would he be?

His eyes were not as sharp as they once had been, he discovered as he followed the trail left by the outlaws. At first, he had no trouble but, as he continued north, he found that, from time to time, he had to rein Abner to a halt, swing down from the saddle, and bend over with his hands on his knees to study the ground more closely. He didn't lose the trail but the days when it would have been as plain as could be for him to see were long gone.

He had been riding for several hours. It had been quite a while since he had spent that much time on horseback and his old bones were really starting to feel it. Maybe he should have ridden with just a blanket, as he had in his youth, he thought, but he had grown accustomed to using a saddle like a white man. He should have known better.

He was thirsty, too. A canteen full of water hung from the saddle horn but Three Horses knew that wasn't what he wanted. When he lifted his hand to wipe the back of it across his mouth, he noticed that it was shaking a little more than it had been back in town, when he had decided to follow the Ranger and the outlaws. Maybe he ought to turn back, he thought. It wasn't too late.

That was when he heard the sharp cracks of rifle fire in the distance ahead of him.

Three Horses brought Abner to a stop and frowned.

He could tell that at least two guns were going off but Braddock hadn't caught up to the whole gang or else the sounds of battle would have been much greater. Still, Three Horses had no doubt that the Ranger was involved in the violent altercation going on somewhere up ahead.

He leaned forward and squinted. Perhaps a quarter of a mile away, he saw some large slabs of rock along the rim. That would be a good place for an ambush, he thought, remembering the days when he had lain in wait in just such a situation, ready to kill any white men unlucky enough to ride by.

Some of the outlaws could have ambushed Ranger Braddock, Three Horses decided. He had no idea where Braddock had taken cover but the lawman had to be alive or else the shooting would have stopped.

He turned the mule toward the rim. It was time for stealth—and no one was stealthier than a Comanche war chief.

He found a cut that led down into the valley at a fairly gentle angle and rode Abner along it for a hundred yards. Then, he stopped and tied the mule's reins to a bush. Taking the Sharps with him, Three Horses started walking along the sloping face of the escarpment, detouring to avoid areas that were too rocky or steep.

He wasn't exactly nimble-footed anymore and almost slipped and fell several times. But he made fairly good progress as the guns continued to blast above him. When he judged that he was almost even with them, he turned and started to climb back toward the rim.

He reached it not far from the rocks he had seen earlier. Staying low, he lifted his head just enough to see two men hidden behind the slabs. One of them had a bloody rag tied around his left thigh as a bandage. Three

Horses smiled a little. Braddock had wounded one of the men trying to kill him.

Three Horses studied the pair for a long moment. They looked familiar and when he was convinced they had been with Clete and Riggs and the other outlaws in Dinsmore that morning, he reached into his pocket and took out one of the long cartridges the Sharps used. These men were cold-blooded killers, and whatever happened to them, they had it coming.

He opened the breech and slid in the cartridge, then closed it and lifted the Sharps to his shoulder. It was heavy and his hands and arms shook from the weight. He had to rest the barrel on a rock to steady the weapon.

Once he had done that, it was easier. He had a good view of both men, so he cocked the rifle and settled the sights on the one who wasn't wounded, figuring he was probably more of a threat because he was uninjured. When he was satisfied with his aim, Three Horses drew in a breath, held it, and squeezed the trigger.

The Sharps boomed and kicked back against his shoulder so hard it knocked him off his feet. He tumbled down the slope behind him, ass over teakettle, as the white men would say.

He had no idea whether or not the .50 caliber round had hit its target. All he could do was try to stop himself from falling and hope his head didn't hit a rock on the way down and bust wide open.

9

WHEN BRADDOCK HEARD THE BUFFALO GUN GO OFF, followed instantly by a shout that might have been pain or surprise or both, his instincts told him this was the only chance he would have to turn the tables on the bushwhackers. One of the rifles started to crack again, fast, as if the man using it was firing as fast as he could work the weapon's lever, and that made up Braddock's mind for him.

One of the bushwhackers was out of action and the other was going after whoever was responsible for that.

Braddock leaped to his feet and raced toward the rocks, zigzagging a little to make himself a more difficult target as his boots pounded the hard ground.

As far as he could tell, nobody shot at him. He had the Winchester held at a slant across his chest with a round in the chamber, ready to go. As he reached the rocks, he darted between two of the big stone slabs and looked around, instantly spotting a man lying on his back with a bloody, fist-sized hole in his chest.

Not much doubt about where the bullet from that

buffalo gun had gone or that the man it had struck was dead.

Shots came from Braddock's right. He looked in that direction, saw a man standing there firing a rifle down the slope at something. The man's instincts must have alerted him to Braddock's presence because he twisted around and tried to bring his rifle to bear on the Ranger.

Braddock's Winchester came up first and cracked as flame spurted from its muzzle. A puff of dust rose from the man's shirt as the bullet punched through the breast pocket and on into his chest. The slug's impact knocked the man back a step and, as he staggered, he lost his footing and fell backwards over the rim.

Braddock rushed over in time to see the man he had shot rolling down the slope. The loose-limbed way the man fell with his arms and legs flopping this way and that told Braddock he was dead.

Braddock didn't see anybody else, and he wondered what the bushwhacker had been shooting at back here—and who had killed the other man. Then he heard a weak voice call, "Ranger!" and spotted movement behind one of the stunted bushes that grew here and there on the escarpment's face.

The old Indian, Three Horses, pulled himself into view and struggled to stand. He propped himself up with an old Sharps carbine, holding on to the barrel with both hands as he rested the stock on the ground. Braddock hoped that antique wasn't loaded now, although he had a pretty good hunch Three Horses had used it to blow that hole in the first bushwhacker.

"Three Horses, what in blazes are you doing here?" Braddock asked.

The Indian grunted and said, "Saving your white hide, Ranger. I could use...a little help."

The old man was breathing hard but, as far as Braddock could see, he was only winded, not wounded. There were no bloodstains on the ragged work clothes.

Braddock moved down the slope, sliding a little in places, and reached Three Horses' side. He grasped the old-timer's upper right arm and steadied him. They began to climb, with Three Horses holding the Sharps barrel in his left hand and using the carbine like a walking stick.

"I reckon that buffalo gun's what I heard go off a few minutes ago," Braddock said.

"Did I hit the man?"

"You blew a big hole right through one of them. And I killed the other one."

"We make a good team," Three Horses said.

Braddock wanted to tell the old Indian they weren't any kind of a team, good or otherwise, but he also knew that Three Horses had helped him out quite a bit. It would be a stretch to say that Three Horses had saved his life because Braddock thought he could have held out until nightfall and dealt with the outlaws then but, this way, he wouldn't have to waste the rest of the day holed up in those rocks. He could go ahead and get after Fenner and the others.

They had reached the top. Braddock still held Three Horses' arm as he nodded toward the dead man and asked, "Did you get a look at them? Were they part of the same bunch that raided Dinsmore?"

"I am certain of it," Three Horses said.

"Then we just whittled them down by twenty-five per cent."

"Yes. The odds against us are better now although we are still outnumbered."

Braddock shook his head and said, "Not us. I don't

know how you got here but you're turning around and going back to Dinsmore."

"My honor is still not satisfied," Three Horses said as he lifted his chin defiantly.

"This isn't about honor. It's about the law. Bringing those men to justice is my job."

"Is it?"

Braddock stiffened. There was no way Three Horses could know that officially he wasn't a Texas Ranger anymore. The old-timer seemed to be pretty canny, though, despite his reputation back in town as a drunkard.

"Look, this is too dangerous for somebody your age—"

"I was not the one who was pinned down," Three Horses said as he looked coolly at Braddock.

"I would have gotten out of that spot."

"Perhaps."

"No maybe about it," Braddock snapped. "Do you have a horse?"

Three Horses hesitated, then said, "A mule."

"Go get it and head back to Dinsmore."

"I will not."

"Then, damn it, if I have to arrest you—"

"Will you take me back yourself and lock me up?" Three Horses smiled. "If you do, the rest of those men will get away from you. You know that."

The worst part about it was that Braddock *did* know that. Three Horses had given him a gift and he was wasting it by standing around here jawing.

"All right," he said. "I guess I can't stop you from going wherever you want to. But I'll be damned if I'm going to wait around for you. You can keep up or not. And if there's more shooting, I won't be looking out for you, either. You'll be on your own and have to keep yourself alive."

"I am not worried. I am the—"

"The last war chief of the Comanches, I know," Braddock said.

He left the rocks and started to walk quickly toward his dun, which was still grazing in the distance. This ambush had already slowed him down enough.

Somewhere up ahead, Clete Fenner and five more outlaws were still on the loose and heaven help anybody whose path happened to cross theirs.

10

Dave Metcalf never got tired of looking at his wife, Sheila. His favorite way to look at her, of course, was when she was undressed like when she was rising out of the big, galvanized bathtub with her creamy skin wet and gleaming or gazing up at her when she was riding him, leaning forward slightly with an intent look on her face and her lower lip caught between her teeth and her thick blond hair hanging down, tickling his chest.

At moments like that, his first thought was about how much he loved her and his second was to wonder how in the world a hardscrabble rancher who admittedly wasn't much to look at had ever talked a gorgeous woman like her into marrying him.

But he liked to look at her when she had her clothes on, too, like now when she came in with the apron she wore over a blue dress lifted and gathered to make a basket for the potatoes and beans and squash she had just gathered from their garden. Through the open door behind her, Dave could see the barn where his two hands, Luis and Clint, were leading in their horses after the day's work.

Dave had been out on the range with them earlier but he had come on in to the house to finish up a letter he was writing so he could take it to Dinsmore and mail it the next day. He was buying some cattle from a rancher over by Callesburg and the letter would finalize the deal.

Also, he had hoped that maybe he and Sheila could go in the bedroom for a spell but she'd been too busy with her own chores, she said, and swatted him away...but with a smile that promised maybe, next time, it would be different.

"Gonna put those vegetables in the stew?" Dave asked his wife as she walked over to the stove where a big iron pot of water was already simmering.

"That's right. Did you finish what you were doing?"

"Got it right here," Dave said as he put his hand on the letter that sat on the rolltop desk in front of him. That desk had belonged to his late father who'd been a professor of natural history at one of the universities back east. Dave hadn't followed him into teaching. He preferred being out living in nature, rather than lecturing about it in some stuffy old building.

He was glad he still had the desk to remind him of his father, though, who had been a kindly man at heart. Hauling it all the way out here by wagon hadn't been easy.

Dave stood up and moved toward Sheila, coming up behind her at the stove. Without looking around, she said, "Don't you go getting any ideas in your head. I'm busy and Luis and Clint will be coming in here in just a few minutes."

"I can't help getting ideas," Dave said. "I just can't do anything about—"

A shot blasted somewhere outside.

The sound made both Dave and Sheila jump a little. Sheila's blue eyes were wide as she looked around and said, "What in the world?"

"One of the boys probably killed a snake," Dave said. "You know how many rattlers there are around here."

A little shudder went through Sheila at the reminder. She said, "I know. I always watch for them."

"I'll go see what happened," Dave said as he started toward the door. He glanced at the rifle and the shotgun hanging on hooks on the other side of the room but decided he wouldn't need either of them. Both of his riders carried belt guns for killing snakes.

He had just stepped through the door when somebody yelled and a gun went off again, then twice more, fast. A scream came from the barn. It sounded like Luis, Dave thought as fear suddenly burst inside him.

"Dave, what—" Sheila exclaimed as he whirled and lunged back into the house toward the weapons. Before he could get there, somebody kicked the back door open and a man rushed in and leveled a revolver at him. Dave skidded to a halt, terribly sure that he was about to die in the next heartbeat.

The man with the gun didn't pull the trigger, though. He just grinned at Dave and said, "Hold it right there, friend. No need for anybody else to get hurt." His eyes flicked toward Sheila for a second and his grin widened as he looked back at Dave. "Your wife?"

"Y-yes," he forced out. "Please, don't shoot. Whatever you want, food, horses, whatever, just take it and leave." He thought about those cattle he'd been planning to buy and went on, "We...we even have some money saved up..."

"Well, ain't that enterprisin' of you. Don't worry,

friend. We'll take it." The intruder looked at Sheila again and added, "We'll take it all."

Despair welled up inside Dave. He knew his pleas meant nothing and so did the man's promise not to hurt them. The man wasn't alone. There were others out in the barn and they had probably killed Luis and Clint by now. They would kill him, too, and they would take what they wanted from Sheila, all of them more than likely, before they killed her and burned the place to the ground. In that instant, Dave saw it all happen inside his head in horrifying detail, the unfolding images so terrible and ugly that he wanted to look away but couldn't.

So if he was doomed anyway, he might as well die fighting, he realized, and if there was even the slightest, tiniest chance that he and Sheila could survive...

All that flashed through his brain in the blink of an eye, and then his muscles tensed for a desperate leap. Before he could move, a step sounded behind him and something crashed against the back of his head.

The blow was enough to knock him to his knees. He felt like his brain was exploding inside his skull. He fell forward, twisting as he collapsed, and it seemed to take forever for him to land on his side on the rough plank floor.

As he did, he saw a man looming over him, gun in hand, and knew he'd been pistol-whipped from behind. The man was tall, broad-shouldered, with an angular, lantern-jawed face under his hat and not even a single ounce of mercy in his cold gray eyes.

Sheila screamed and bolted toward Dave. The man who had come in the back door hurriedly jammed his gun back in its holster and caught her, pulling her away as he wrapped his arms around her, pinning them to her sides. She kicked at him but he swung her off the floor so that her struggles were futile.

"This fella was getting ready to jump you, Riggs," the second man said. "You were too busy looking at the woman to notice, weren't you? You're lucky I came in when I did."

"Ah, hell, Clete, you worry too much. I had the drop on him. If he'd come at me, I'd have shot him. It's better this way, though. He ain't dead, is he?"

Dave barely felt it as a boot toe prodded his side but it was enough to make him moan.

"He's alive."

"Good. That way he can watch what we do to his pretty little wife. That'll be a show, won't it?"

"Later," Clete said. "After she's fixed some supper for us. I don't know about you but I'm hungry."

"Yeah," Riggs said as he buried his face in Sheila's hair and laughed. "I'm damn near starvin'."

11

A THIN THREAD OF SMOKE, ALMOST INVISIBLE AGAINST THE fading light in the sky, was the first indication something was ahead of them. Braddock had pulled the dun back to a walk to rest the horse when he spotted the smoke. He turned his head to look over his shoulder at Three Horses who was about twenty feet behind him on the mule.

"I see it, too," the Indian said, somehow knowing what Braddock had been about to point out. "I saw it before you did, Ranger."

"Fine," Braddock said. "It doesn't matter who saw it first. Do you know where it's coming from?"

Three Horses said, "There are ranches up here. The people who live on them come into Dinsmore sometimes. But I do not know their names. They never had anything to do with me except to look at me with pity or disgust as they passed on the street."

Braddock grunted. The old-timer sure liked to wallow in his misery. But he didn't have the right to make any judgments, Braddock told himself. He had done some wallowing, too, back in the days after Captain Hughes had told him he wasn't a Ranger anymore. Before he'd decided that it didn't matter what anybody else said: he would always be a Ranger.

Braddock stopped and waited for Three Horses to catch up to him. He said, "That's chimney smoke. Got to be from a ranch house. Fenner and his bunch likely saw it, too."

"Perhaps they went around, to avoid being spotted."

"Maybe...but it's more likely they stopped to loot the place."

And kill whoever lives there, Braddock added to himself.

Three Horses seemed to be thinking the same thing. He said, "The rancher and his family are in danger."

"Yeah. If they're still alive. But if they are and we go busting in there without knowing the situation, it's liable to just make things worse for them."

"You need a scout," Three Horses said.

"I need to have a look-see for myself. You're going to stay here."

"You agreed to let me help."

"I did no such thing," Braddock said. "I told you I couldn't stop you from riding wherever you wanted to. But now I'm going to. You go stumbling around that bunch, you'll ruin everything."

Three Horses drew himself up straight in the saddle and gave Braddock a haughty look. He said stubbornly, "I will ride with you until we see what there is to see. Then...maybe I will wait."

That was probably the only concession he would get, thought Braddock. The old-timer's treatment at the hands of the outlaws had stung his pride so badly that he was determined to get his revenge, no matter what the cost. Braddock couldn't let that interfere with his job but he supposed he could let it slide for the moment.

When the time came, he could tie and gag the old man if he had to, to make him stay put.

They rode on. The sun had just dipped below the horizon when they came in sight of several buildings sticking up from the plains. Braddock reined in and dismounted, motioning for Three Horses to do likewise. Out here on this flat land, the taller you were, the more visible you were.

Braddock had a pair of field glasses in his saddlebags. There was still enough light in the sky for him to see as he peered through the lenses.

The barn was the only structure built of planks since lumber was at a premium out here on these mostly tree-less plains. The main house and smaller bunkhouse were built of sod or adobe, Braddock couldn't tell which at this distance. He could see there were more than half a dozen horses in the corral next to the barn, though. That was a bad sign. The animals might not belong to Fenner and his gang, but chances were they did.

Three Horses tapped him on the shoulder. Braddock lowered the glasses and said, "What?"

The Indian pointed into the sky to the right of the barn. Braddock's eyes narrowed as he saw the dark shapes circling there, riding the gentle wind currents. He lifted the glasses again and squinted through them.

"There's something out there," he said a moment later. "Hard to tell for sure. It might be a couple of bodies, though."

"The carrion eaters will descend soon. They know death when they see it."

"Yeah." Braddock tracked the glasses back to the barn. Movement caught his eye. Two men stood in the barn's open doorway, gesturing as they talked. He saw the tiny orange specks that were the glowing ends of the quirlies they smoked. The men were roughly dressed, unshaven. Braddock knew outlaws when he saw them.

"It's Fenner and his gang, all right," he said. "They've killed a couple of people already. They dragged the carcasses out away from the barn. There are two men still there in front of the barn, probably keeping an eye on things."

"So four in the house," Three Horses said.

"More than likely." Braddock stowed the field glasses. "I need to get around behind the place and approach it from that angle. If I ride in from this way, they'll see me coming for sure." He looked at his companion. "You have to give me your word that you'll stay here."

Three Horses got that stubborn look on his wrinkled face again.

"They attacked the honor of a Comanche war chief," he said as if that explained everything.

"Damn it, Pete, if you don't give me your word, I'll—"

He didn't have to finish the threat. The old-timer raised his hand to stop him, sighed, and said, "Very well. You have my word. I will stay here and not interfere."

That was almost too easy, Braddock thought as he frowned. Maybe he ought to make sure and tie up the old fella anyway.

On the other hand, if he wound up dying this evening, Three Horses would be stuck here, tied up and unable to get away. He might be able to work himself loose eventually but what if he wasn't? What if a rattlesnake came crawling along while the old-timer couldn't do anything about it?

And if the outlaws killed him, thought Braddock, there was a good chance they would look around to see if anyone else was in the area. They might find the Indian and then Lord knew what they would do to him...

"All right, blast it. I'm going to have to take you at your word. I hope I can count on it."

Three Horses just folded his arms across his chest and gazed serenely at the Ranger.

"I'll come back and get you once I've dealt with those varmints," Braddock promised. "And if I don't come back, you head for Dinsmore. You can bring Deputy Bell and a posse back out here and pick up the trail again." He added grimly, "And bury anybody who needs burying."

Without waiting for Three Horses to respond, Braddock moved off to the east on foot, leading the dun. It was less likely the outlaws would spot him if he came in from that direction, rather than skylighting himself against the remaining light in the west. The edge of the Caprock was at least a mile away now, so he had plenty of room to do that.

As he moved into position, he wondered if Fenner and the others were getting curious about the two men they had left behind. Maybe, maybe not. They might not expect those two to rejoin them until later in the night or even in the morning. With their back trail covered like that, they might not be expecting trouble. Braddock hoped that was the case and that they wouldn't be quite as alert as a result.

With six-to-one odds, he would take any slight advantage he could get.

It took him about twenty minutes to get around the ranch headquarters and reach a spot half a mile north of the buildings. He left the dun there and started toward the place on foot, carrying the rifle and moving in a low crouch. He figured the outlaws wouldn't be expecting any trouble from this direction but it never hurt to be careful.

Or rather, it *seldom* hurt to be careful, Braddock mused.

Sometimes, a man just had to take a wild-ass chance.

BRADDOCK CRAWLED THE LAST COUPLE OF HUNDRED yards, using the scrub brush for cover. This was the time of day rattlesnakes came out but luck was with him and he encountered only a couple of the creatures. The snakes didn't coil up either time but slithered off in disdain, instead.

As far as he could see, Fenner hadn't posted any guards in back of the house. Braddock was able to crawl to within a few yards of the structure which, he could tell now, was made from thick blocks of adobe. The back door was closed but windows were on either side of it. He came up on one knee, then onto his feet and stole forward.

Glass panes were set in both windows. That probably cost the rancher quite a bit but it made the place look nicer. Curtains hung on the inside of the glass but they were pushed aside so that Braddock could see through. He checked the one to the left of the door first. It opened into a bedroom that was empty at the moment. Braddock could see the big four-poster bed in the dim light. The door to the rest of the house was closed.

He slid along the rear wall, past the door, and took off his hat as he edged his eye past the side of the other window.

This one gave him a view of the ranch house's large main room which included both the kitchen and a living area. The place was furnished in what appeared to be functional but comfortable fashion with a good-sized table that had four ladderback chairs around it, a fireplace with a couple of rocking chairs near it, and a rolltop desk with another ladderback chair. Woven rugs were scattered on the plank floor.

A dark-haired man lay on his side on one of those rugs in an awkward position because his arms were pulled behind his back and his wrists were lashed together. His ankles were bound as well. He was conscious but seemed groggy as if he didn't quite know what was going on around him.

Braddock knew, though. He saw the four men sitting at the table with bowls of what looked like stew in front of them. They had torn hunks off a loaf of fresh bread, too, and were eating hungrily. Braddock recognized Clete Fenner right away from wanted posters he had seen. The others looked familiar as well, so he was sure their faces had decorated plenty of reward dodgers.

A very attractive blond woman stood beside the table. She wore a blue dress and a white apron, both of which were somewhat disheveled as if the men had been pawing her. Braddock didn't doubt that was what happened. She looked scared, as she had every right to be, but she looked angry, too.

The woman started to move away from the table but

the man closest to her reached out and closed his hand around her wrist.

"You know better than that, honey," he told her. Braddock had no trouble understanding the words because the window was raised a few inches to let fresh air into the room. "You need to stay right here close in case one of us needs anything. You don't wanna be rude to your guests, now do you?"

Fenner looked up with an expression of mild interest on his lean face. He asked, "What were you about to do, Mrs. Metcalf?"

The blonde said, "I have a pie over there in the keeper. I thought you might want some of it."

"Sounds good," Fenner said. "Riggs, go with her. Make sure she's not trying any sort of trick."

"No trick," the woman said. "It's just peach pie."

The outlaw called Riggs grinned and said, "That does sound mighty good. Let's you and me get it, honey. That'll just whet my appetite for more sweetness with you later on."

Braddock recalled that Riggs was one of the men who'd struck Three Horses back in Dinsmore, just before the gang hit the bank. The woman didn't respond to the veiled threat in the outlaw's voice. With Riggs beside her, she crossed the room to a pie keeper that sat on a shelf and opened it to take out the peach pie.

For a second, Braddock thought she was about to ram the pie tin into Riggs' face and he was ready to move if she did so. He would have no choice but to kick the back door open, go in shooting, and hope for the best.

But then the fury he had seen on the woman's face disappeared as she regained control of her emotions and she turned placidly back to the table, holding the pie in both hands. Riggs didn't seem to have noticed what had almost happened.

Outside the window, Braddock relaxed slightly. He wouldn't have to make his move just yet, although he knew that his time was running out fast.

What he needed was some sort of distraction, something that would draw the four killers out of the house. Then he could go in fast while the woman escaped out the back, and take them from behind. With any luck, he could drop a couple of them before they knew what was going on, and then he would take his chances with the others.

He was still trying to figure out what that distraction might be when one of the men from the barn appeared in the open front door and said, "Clete, you got to see this."

Fenner looked up and asked, "What is it? Are Chuck and Gardner here already?"

Chuck and Gardner—those would be the two men who'd ambushed him, thought Braddock.

The man at the door shook his head and said, "No, but it's something I've never seen before."

Mrs. Metcalf set the pie on the table as Fenner stood up impatiently. As he started toward the door, he said, "All right, but this better be worth it, Gant."

"Oh, it is," Gant said.

Curious, the other men stood up and started to follow Fenner. The boss outlaw glanced back and snapped, "Riggs, you stay here and keep an eye on the woman and her husband."

"Ah, hell, Clete—" Riggs began.

"Just do it."

Riggs shrugged and smiled at the blonde, saying, "I don't care what's out there anyway. I'd rather spend my time with you, darlin'." He ran a hand up her arm and slid his fingers along the line of her jaw before cupping her chin.

Braddock ducked down to move below the window as he eased over to the rear corner of the ranch house. He was just as curious as the others about what the man called Gant had spotted. He wasn't expecting what he saw.

Sitting out there on the back of his mule a hundred yards away, dressed in full Comanche regalia, including beaded buckskins and a tall, feathered headdress, was Three Horses. He held the Sharps carbine with the stock propped against his right thigh so the barrel pointed at the sky. With the light behind him, he was a pretty impressive figure. He would have been more impressive on a Comanche pony instead of a mule but a fella' had to work with what he had available.

The five outlaws were at the edge of Braddock's view, partially concealed by the building as they stood there staring at Three Horses. A couple of them laughed but one man said with a nervous edge in his voice, "I didn't think there were any savage Indians still around, Clete. I thought they were all up in Oklahoma these days."

"That's not a savage Indian," Fenner said disdainfully. "That's just a crazy old man. In fact...Riggs, come out here. I think that old redskin from Dinsmore must have followed us."

Braddock whirled back to the window. He had wanted a distraction and Three Horses, despite breaking his word, had given him one. If Riggs would just leave the woman inside, Braddock could get in there, free her and her husband, and then hell could go ahead and start to pop.

Riggs wasn't going to leave the woman, though. He

168

grasped her upper left arm to drag her along with him as he said, "Come on, honey. Killin' an old Injun ought to be some good sport. Get me nice and worked up for you, later on."

They had taken a couple of steps when the blonde reached under her apron with her free hand, brought out a small pistol from somewhere, and jammed the barrel against the side of Riggs' head as she pulled the trigger. The gun went off with a little pop, not loud at all, and Riggs staggered. Braddock knew a small-caliber slug like that would bounce around inside a man's skull and turn his brain into mush.

Around on the other side of the cabin, Three Horses kicked the mule into a run, let out a high-pitched whoop, and charged through the dusk.

Since Braddock was closer to the door than the corner, he booted it open and ran inside. Riggs had collapsed to leak blood onto the floor from the bullet hole in his head but Mrs. Metcalf was on her feet and swung the little revolver in her hand toward the stranger who had just burst into her house.

"Texas Ranger!" Braddock called out so she wouldn't shoot him, too. "Stay with your husband and stay down!"

He reached the doorway in time to see the other five outlaws starting to scatter as startled exclamations came from them. They clawed out their revolvers but Three Horses was still out of range of the handguns.

The outlaws weren't out of range of the Sharps, though. Somehow the old-timer found the strength to fire it on the run, its heavy boom rolling through the twilight. Braddock knew the shot wasn't going to hit anything—

That thought had just gone through his brain when an outlaw's head flew apart like a dropped pumpkin. Lucky shot or not, the man was just as dead either way.

With everything that was going on, the remaining desperadoes hadn't noticed Braddock yet. Normally, he would have called on them in the name of the State of Texas, ordering them to drop their guns, elevate, and surrender.

But with all the blood these men had on their hands, he didn't hesitate to bring the Winchester to his shoulder and open fire.

Sharp cracks split the air as he drilled two of the outlaws and sent them spinning off their feet. Fenner and the remaining man were triggering at the still charging Three Horses who continued to whoop madly as he galloped toward them.

Three Horses was in range now and he jerked back as lead found him. He couldn't stay on the mule. He slid sideways and then pitched off.

Braddock planted a slug between the shoulder blades of the fifth man, knocking him forward onto his face where he landed in a limp sprawl.

That left Fenner and he moved with the speed that had kept him alive for this long in his perilous career as a badman. He whirled toward Braddock and got a shot off, coming close enough that Braddock felt the heat of the bullet as it whipped past his ear.

Then Braddock slammed three rounds into Fenner's chest as fast as he could work the Winchester's lever and the outlaw went over backward. With his arms outflung, he writhed in the dust for a second, arching his back, then died with one leg drawn up and the knee cocked at the sky, where stars were beginning to appear against the deep blue in the east.

Braddock levered another cartridge into the Winchester's chamber, just in case, then slowly lowered the rifle. He looked at the bodies scattered all around.

"Are...are they all dead?" Mrs. Metcalf asked from the door behind him.

"I'm pretty sure they are," Braddock replied. "But pretty sure isn't good enough."

He went from body to body, making certain that they were, indeed, corpses. He was tempted to put a few more bullets in them, just for good measure, but he figured he would have enjoyed that too much. He looked at Mrs. Metcalf and nodded instead, to let her know she was safe now.

She looked at the pistol in her hand and said, "I carry it for snakes."

"I'd say that's how you used it," Braddock said.

"I'm surprised none of them found it while they were pawing me. I guess they were too careless. Or they weren't meant to find it."

Things like that were beyond Braddock's reckoning. He told the woman, "Stay here and take care of your husband," then started walking toward the fallen figure of Three Horses.

By the time he got there, he was running.

He slid to a stop, dropped to one knee, and rolled the old Indian onto his back. There was a dark stain on the buckskin shirt, high on the right side.

Three Horses grunted and said, "Be careful. I've been shot."

"I can see that," Braddock said, surprisingly grateful to find that the old man was alive. "You gave me your word you'd stay out of this."

"Old Pete gave you his word. Three Horses, the last war chief of the Comanche, did not." He sighed. "Are our enemies all dead?"

"Every last one of them."

"This is good. The honor of the Comanche people has

been avenged, at least this one last time." Another sigh came from the old man. "I see stars above me. They welcome me to the realm of the spirits. It is a good day to die."

Three Horses' eyes closed.

"Die, hell," Braddock said. "Unless all your blood's dried up so that you don't have any to spare, you'll be fine. Looks like that bullet went straight through without doing much damage."

Three Horses opened one eye and said, "Really?"

"Really," Braddock told him. "Let's get you on your feet. If you can walk to that ranch house, there's a lady there who I'll bet can patch you up. She's got some peach pie, too."

"Peach pie," Three Horses repeated.

"I thought that might get you moving," Braddock said.

He helped the old man to his feet, carried the rifle in his left hand, and put his left arm around Three Horses' waist to support him as they walked slowly toward the ranch house where both of the Metcalfs waited now.

"You had all this get-up in that carpetbag you carry around, didn't you?"

"This get-up, as you call it, is the way a Comanche war chief should dress."

"Maybe so. I'll admit, it looks all right on you."

"Is there...a reward...for those men?"

"Sure. I expect it'll add up to quite a bit. If I was you, I'd share it with these folks. They deserve something for what they've gone through and, anyway, it was the lady who killed Riggs."

Three Horses sighed and said, "I would have liked to kill him myself. But I am glad he is dead. He had it coming."

"No argument from me," Braddock said.

After a moment, the old man asked, "You are not going to stay and claim any of the reward?"

"No, now that it's all over and justice has been done, I have to move on."

"Of course. The hole in your badge. Some things appear true and are false. Some things appear false and are true."

"You talking about the two of us or just spouting philosophy like a dime novel Indian?"

Instead of answering, Three Horses asked, "Have you ever thought about having someone to ride along with you on your journeys?"

"Like Natty Bumppo and Chingachgook, you mean?"

Three Horses snorted and said, "Someone has to get you out of trouble, white man."

Braddock shook his head and said, "That's not happening in a million years," as they limped on slowly through the dusk.

ABOUT THE AUTHOR

James Reasoner has been telling tales and spinning yarns as far back as he can remember. He's been doing it professionally for more than 40 years, and during that time, under his own name and dozens of pseudonyms, he's written almost 400 novels and more than 100 shorter pieces of fiction. His books have appeared on the *New York Times, USA Today,* and *Publishers Weekly* bestseller lists. He has written Westerns, mysteries, historical sagas, war novels, science fiction and fantasy, and horror fiction.

Growing up in the late Fifties and early Sixties when every other series on television was a Western made him into a lifelong fan of the genre. The Lone Ranger, Roy Rogers, Hopalong Cassidy, Matt Dillon, and John Wayne made quite an impression on him. At the age of 10, he discovered Western novels when he checked out *Single Jack* by Max Brand and *Hopalong Cassidy* (there's that name again!) by Clarence E. Mulford from the library bookmobile that came out every Saturday to the small town in Texas where he lived. He's been reading Westerns ever since, long before he started writing them, and always will.

James Reasoner has also written numerous articles, essays, and book introductions on a variety of topics related to popular culture, including vintage paperbacks and the publishing industry, pulp magazines, comics, movies, and TV. He writes the popular blog *Rough*

Edges and is the founder and moderator of an email group devoted to Western pulp magazines.

He lives in the same small town in Texas where he grew up and is married to the popular mystery novelist Livia J. Washburn, who has also written Westerns under the name L.J. Washburn.